THE

Convent School,

OR

EARLY EXPERIENCES

OF

A YOUNG FLAGELLANT.

———————

BY ROSA BELINDA COOTE.

———————

BIRCHGROVE PRESS.
2015

The Convent School, or Early Experiences of a Young Flagellant.
By Rosa Belinda Coote.

Miss Coote's Confession, or The Voluptuous Experiences
of an Old Maid

© Birchgrove Press
2015

ISBN:
978-0-9923919-2-8

Ostensibly written by Rosa Belinda Coote, *The Convent School, or Early Experiences of a Young Flagellant* was actually written and published by William Lazenby, a notorious and enigmatic publisher of Victorian clandestine erotica. It was first published in London in 1879 in a limited edition of 150 copies and sold for the then exorbitant sum of £3 3s.

This Birchgrove Press edition includes *The Convent School's* companion volume, *Miss Coote's Confession, or The Voluptuous Experiences of an Old Maid*, which was also written by Lazenby. It was published in instalments in Lazenby's *The Pearl: A Journal of Facetiæ and Voluptuous Reading* (July 1879 to April 1880 issues). The ten letters that compose the text were later collected and published by 'THE SOCIETY OF VICE' in a volume dated 1892.

THE

CONVENT SCHOOL

THE

Convent School,

OR

EARLY EXPERIENCES

OF

A YOUNG FLAGELLANT.

BY ROSA BELINDA COOTE.

BIRCHGROVE PRESS.
2015

Salomon said, in accents mild,
Spare the rod and spoil the child;
Be they man or be they maid,
Whip and wallop'em, Salomon said

The dicta of the Wise Man concerning discipline have been the source of inexpressible dolour to children for very many centuries; and it has only been within the last sixty years that ferocity in the treatment of infants (I am speaking of English children, Jean Jacques Rousseau shamed the French out of the practice of beating their offspring, nearly a hundred years ago) has been gradually diminishing. In the eighteenth century the lot of the British juvenile was certainly a cruel one. That admirable woman, the mother of the Wesleys, held that a child should be made to desist from crying and to "fear the rod" at the mature age of twelve months; and Miss Maria Semple, writing on education in 1812, tells a story of a lady who was educated in early years by a relative, "On a certain day in every week she received corporal punishment. If she had committed faults, 'the punishment was due;' if she had not, she probably would in the week ensuing. At the distance of more than half-a-century, the memory of this person, who bore a public character of piety and virtue, was spoken of, and justly, with aversion by the person she had thus treated." Thus Miss Maria Semple.—"G. A. S.," in the *Illustrated London News*.

INTRODUCTORY LETTER

OF

THE AUTHORESS.

My Dear Nellie,—

Since writing you my confession, in that series of letters which you flattered me by calling "most interesting facts, and deliciously voluptuous reading for lovers of the rod," the following curious narrative has been entrusted to my confidential keeping by a young Countess of my acquaintance; but as there are no secrets between us, and I think it may afford some little pleasure in the perusal, I hasten to copy it out for you, from notes which I made day by day at the bedside of the dear young creature, as she told the particulars to me, at my visits during her long and painful illness, now, I am afraid, close upon a fatal termination; and you may guess how grieved I am to think that, although I now reserve her name as a secret, too solemn to be entrusted, even to you, the stillness of the grave will soon do away with all necessity for such reticence. Should my confessions ever be printed after our time, this tale certainly ought to bear them company, either as prefix or addenda.

Believe me, dear Nellie,
Your ever affectionate friend,
ROSA BELINDA COOTE.
London, 10th January, 1825.

THE CONVENT SCHOOL,

OR

EARLY EXPERIENCES

OF

A YOUNG FLAGELLANT

—————

CHAPTER I

The Early Life of Lucille

Since, dear Rosie, you are so interested to hear my birching and whipping experiences, I will try to recollect them as well as possible, but hope you will consider my weak state of health, and not press me to tell you too much at once.

Perhaps you do not know that almost from my infancy it was arranged that I should marry the Earl of Ellington, who was about twelve years my senior, being a family compact of a purely mercenary character, designed to consolidate some very doubtful title deeds, which now that our union has proved unfruitful, are likely to entail great expense and annoyance to our heirs-at-law.

My father, you know, was the Honourable Mr. Warton, and my mother died in giving birth to myself, so that I was brought up under a nurse, and afterwards, when about seven years old, a young lady was engaged as governess to instil my juvenile mind with the rudiments of learning, preparatory to being sent to a finishing school.

This lady's name was Miss Birch, and although my papa had known her father, Dr. Birch, for some years, I now believe that the fascination of her name had great influence with him in making a selection from the numerous, and in many instances more eligible ladies, who applied for the situation.

Miss Birch was a dark lady about thirty years of age when she entered our family, very good-looking, rather large pouting mouth, set off with lovely rows of most pearly white teeth, which, when she smiled or said much showed to beautiful effect in contrast to her rather swarthy complexion, dark brown eyes, and thick bushy black arching eyebrows, her figure was well moulded and plump, and being about five feet six, she had quite a commanding presence.

I was nearly eight years old before I began to notice the significant looks which occasionally passed between papa and governess, but hints were so often thrown out about the necessity of procuring a good birch rod for the naughty bottom of Lucille, that I was gradually awakened to the discovery of some most mysterious kind of understanding which must subsist between them. My infant brain was much puzzled and alarmed, as I already felt in imagination the tingling smart of the green twigs I so much dreaded.

Miss Birch seemed more exacting and severe over my lessons, especially when papa happened to be in the schoolroom, and now I will tell you my first experience of the rod.

One day after failing both in spelling and arithmetic she rang the bell, and ordered the servant to request Mr. Warton's presence in the schoolroom for a few minutes. Papa entered with a very serious look, requesting Miss Birch to inform him of the cause of sending for him.

"Mr. Warton," said my governess, "you know we have had many serious conversations about the necessity for proper corrections in case Miss Lucille should continue so inattentive to her studies, to-day she has failed in everything, and I am certain that unless her energies are sharpened up by the stinging smart of the rod she will go from bad to worse; I am so averse to wield the birch myself, and would much prefer that her papa should take in hand the serious whipping she ought to have."

PAPA.—"Lucille, you hear what Miss Birch says, (I noticed him cast most excited and amorous looks towards the governess as he spoke), she has been most forbearing with you, and interceded with me many times to save your bottom, and even now cannot bring herself to lift her own hand to make you smart a little; it must indeed be a serious fault to induce her to ask me to use the rod, but, 'Spare the rod and spoil the child,' has always been a maxim with me; lay her across your lap, Miss Birch, and pull up her clothes, whilst I get the rod out of the table drawer."

MISS BIRCH, with heaving bosom, and quite a deep blush upon her face,—"I feel as ashamed at baring her naughty posteriors as if I was going to suffer the degradation and humiliation myself, but come, Lucille dear, you must bear it, and I hope you will be a better and more diligent girl in future." Then catching me by the wrist, as I stood by her side covered with confusion, she tried to lay me across her knees, but I struggled and screamed, "No! No!! No!!! I won't be whipped! Oh! Oh!! dear papa, do forgive me this time!" my face quite crimson and streaming with tears.

PAPA, having got out the rod, a fine switch of long thin birch twigs, tied up with velvet and silk ribbons at the handle,— "Come! Come!! Lucille, this resistance will only make it worse for you." As he seized and threw me on the governess's lap, Miss Birch securing my head well under her left arm, speedily pulled up dress and skirts, till my fat little bottom was exposed in a tight fitting pair of drawers, my legs being left to kick about, although I was quite firmly secured, and to all intents quite helpless, and my toes could scarcely touch the ground.

I could hear papa whisking the birch about, and then he said, "That will do famously, Miss Birch, keep her head and shoulders well down as you hold up her skirts; much as I pity my darling little Lucille, I must do my duty and make her smart for her idleness in school."

My face was burning hot with the deep blushes of shame, and I struggled desperately to free my head from the vice-like pressure of Miss Birch's arm, as I begged with piteous sobs to be let off for this once. "Oh! dear papa! Oh! pray don't beat me!"

PAPA.—"Indeed, I must, though every blow will send a pang to my own heart, you naughty, bad, inattentive girl, all this has come by your great idleness, and trusting too much to the kind heart of your governess." As he said this, three sharp stinging cuts whacked on my tight-fitting drawers in quick succession.

The pain was intense, I kicked, writhed and screamed for "Mercy! Mercy! Oh! Oh!! I will be good! Oh! Papa! Oh, Miss Birch, do let me go!"

PAPA, in quite an excited tone, (for I could see nothing), "So you mean to be good in future! Do you feel the birch is doing you good already? Ha! ha!! my little Lucille, you must have a little more yet to make a perfect cure of your idleness." Whack—whack—whack—whack—four more cuts, each one more agonizing than the last, in spite of my sobbing and screaming. "Now, Miss Birch," he continued, "let her feel it on the bare flesh, open her drawers so we can see the effects of the cuts."

This was at once done, as I cried, "Ah! Ah!! No! No!! Oh, Papa! How cruel!"

PAPA.—"What a sight. The rod has made her bottom blush finely. It's best to make her feel sore a few days, or she will soon forget it, and relapse into her old ways."

The drawers were unbuttoned, and I could feel they were quite pulled down my thighs, exposing the entire surface of my smarting rump, but I had only a few moments for reflection before the blows fell again in rapid succession, cutting, tearing, and scratching the skin, whilst the boiling blood in my veins seemed to throb as if it must spurt through the pores at every burning touch of the rod.

My head was pressed against the tumultuously heaving bosom of my governess, and notwithstanding the intensity of my suffering,

I could plainly hear the beating of her heart, and knew that her thighs were tightly compressed together, whilst a strange tremor pervaded her entire frame.

"There, there, that will do," said Papa, in a very excited tone. "I've drawn the blood for her. Now, Miss Dunce, kneel and kiss the rod, and ask your governess to forgive you."

I slipped down on my knees and hiding my face in my hands in her lap, promised Miss Birch "if she would forgive me now, to be a better girl in future."

"That will do. I don't want to be too hard upon Lucille this time. We will leave her to think over her disgrace and shame, and let her beware of the birch again," said Papa, taking Miss Birch's hand, to lead her from the room. "This has been a most agitating scene for your governess, who must repose in her private room for a while to recover herself."

The schoolroom door, which opened directly into her private room, was closed upon me, and the key turned in the lock, but all my hurts and bruises were insufficient to distract my attention from the peculiarly warm and excited glances which passed from papa towards my governess, whose face was suffused with blushes, and her eyes turned down, as if afraid to meet his ardent looks as they passed from the room.

My curiosity was excited so much, that I listened at the key-hole. Papa was evidently remaining in the governess's room. I could hear a rustling of her dress, as if some little struggle was taking place: a sound of smothered kisses, and soft expostulatory ejaculations, such as "I dare not! Oh! No! No!! Not now! Pray leave me! Oh! Oh!!" Then an almost perfect quiet, except for a slight rustling sound, and, now and then, broken sighs with heavy breathing.

At last all was quiet, and having now been left more than half-an-hour to myself in the schoolroom, I ventured to tap at the door and beg Miss Birch to let me into her room, as I would never, never, offend again.

After a very slight delay, the door was unlocked, and my governess received me with expressions of great tenderness, kissed her poor Lucille, and hoped my poor bottom was not too sore. Her eyes were melting with what I should now call a soft voluptuous languor, and scintillated with extraordinary brilliancy, all of which set my young ideas in a flutter of wonderment, as to the extraordinary cause of her prolonged emotion.

Things went on pretty smoothly for some time, but I found it quite impossible to avoid coming under the rod every now and then, the chastisement getting more severe on every fresh occasion.

Papa always had to handle the twigs, and when I began to get older, Miss Birch would tie me up and leave the room, as she pretended to be quite unable to bear the scene. Still papa would always go into her sanctum at the conclusion of my whipping, to talk the matter over with my governess.

I will tell you of a fearful birching, the last I had before being sent to the Convent School: it does not matter what the fault was, but it must have been something very serious. Papa and Miss Birch both helped to tie me up on a four-poster bed in my own room. I was stripped of every thing but my skirts and drawers, which were all secured and arranged so as to expose my back parts in the best possible manner for whipping. My hands were tied to the bed post high above my head, and making me kneel on the bed, one leg was secured at the knee to the same post, my other leg being left free to kick about.

Miss Birch vanished, and papa arming himself with a formidable rod, elegantly trimmed as usual, began by lecturing me on my fault.

"You impudent girl, I can scarcely believe it of you, Lucille, now you are just upon twelve, but this is the last whipping you will get at my hands, and I promise you it shall be a sound one, and then I'll pack you off to the convent, with instructions to the sisters to be very strict in looking after you."

"Oh! Oh!! Papa," I implored, "Have mercy, don't be so severe, indeed I won't do it again!"

"Hold your tongue, Miss," he said, impatiently, "you always cry before you are hurt, but you shall remember this whipping as long as you live;" giving me a slashing cut round my loins, then another, and another on each cheek of my buttocks, "how do you like it, you bad girl! will you turn over a new leaf when you leave home? Will you? Will you? Will you? Will you?" Each question being accompanied by a terrific smarter: the blows seemed to cut like a red hot knife, and my boiling blood tingled from the tips of my fingers to the ends of my toes. I could feel great burning bursting weals rising on my skin at every cut: I screamed and plunged till the bed-post creaked with the strain, and my wrists and knee were quite pained by the tight ligatures by which they were secured.

"Let this be a solemn warning to you, Miss Lucille," he continued, "but I'm afraid all my efforts for your reformation are quite thrown away upon such a worthless baggage," cutting away still more ferociously, and as I turned my head to scream and implore for mercy, I could see how excited he was over the business with flushed face and sparkling eyes: he was a fine handsome man of about forty-five, and gave me the idea of looking as if in the midst of a tremendous battle.

Anything but a bloodless battle for me: my bottom was soon dripping with the ruby drops of my young blood, the sight of which seemed only to exasperate him still more.

"Ah! You little wretch. Scream away!" he exclaimed. "It's a beautiful sight to see you writhing and plunging under every scathing cut. May it do you good, and draw the imprudence out of your tail. Will you? Will you, try and behave better, or shall I send you off to the convent at once, in their holiday time? There! There!! There!!!"

He finished with three tremendous cuts, without waiting for my reply, and sank back, gasping for breath, into an easy chair.

It was quite a minute or two before my screams and moans of agony subsided. Then Miss Birch coming in, released my hands and leg, and ordering me to rest on the bed for a while, retired with my father locking the door behind them.

The smarting sensation now turned to a delicious voluptuous warmth, as I lay under the bed clothes. My right hand was passed all over the glowing surface of my buttocks, and seemed at last, quite unwittingly to settle itself on my hairless little cunny. I turned on my belly with my hand still under me and wriggling myself about, as I lay thinking over all the cuts I had received, gradually found a most pleasing sensation from the rubbing of my hand and the two forefingers mechanically worked into the slit, squeezing my legs together, I rubbed on to increase the pleasurable emotions which I felt driving me to strive and obtain, I knew not what. The frenzy now threw me into such a state of excitement that my fingers were plunged as far as possible up my virgin cunny, as I gasped, writhed, and tossed my bottom up and down. The crisis came at last, and my furious efforts were rewarded by a most heavenly emission: my soul seemed to flow from me at the moment, and left me in a delightful state of voluptuous lethargy, which lasted for some minutes, and when at length I regained my serenity, it was to find my fingers, cunny, and thighs all sticky from the thick spermy emission of my first maiden spend. There was also a slight stain of blood, for I had actually ravished myself in my furious excitement.

I got up and sponged myself, then lay down to reflect on the curious and delicious emotions I had procured for myself, and determining to soon have a repetition of my secret joys, fell asleep to dream of being in the arms of a most lovely boy about my own age, who seemed to impart to my ravished senses another taste of what I had already felt.

Awaking in a struggle to retain my love-bird, I found myself bedewed by another emission, but at last I slept with tranquillity, and never shall I forget my first taste of joy that day.

CHAPTER II.

The Convent School

My father's extreme severity made me rather glad when in about a week's time Miss Birch began to make preparations for my departure to Belgium, and in less than three weeks I found myself installed as a pupil in the seminary of the Ursuline nuns at Brussels. The Lady Superior struck me from the very first as being a frightfully severe woman; the morning after my arrival she sent for me to hear her read my father's instructions and remarked that he had given her *carte blanche* as to punishment, and that in their school discipline was strictly enforced. "Remember, young lady," said she, in dismissing me from her presence, "we never overlook a fault, and that my word is law here."

My face flushed with indignation, and tears filled my eyes as I left the apartment, fully assured in my own mind that I must soon experience a taste of their discipline, nor had I long to wait, for two days after, having confidentially expressed my disgust to another pupil, with respect to the coarse fare set before us at meals, I soon found I had been talking to a tell-tale spy, who carried everything to the Superior.

An elderly nun quietly told me she had been sent to conduct me to the private room of the Lady Superior. My time was come, and I followed my chaperone with trembling anxiety.

Our Superior was a stern looking woman of about forty-five, with dark piercing eyes and Roman nose, thin compressed lips considerably adding to the severity of her expression.

"Mdlle. Lucille," said the Superior, "I thought the caution I gave you on your arrival, would at least have saved you from trouble for some time, and spared me the pain of inflicting personal correction on you so soon after your entry into our seminary, but I am afraid your papa must have had serious cause for wishing me to be severe with you; now what have you been saying to your fellow pupil the Mdlle. Olive; did you remark, "that the food was not fit for a dog, much less schoolgirls?"

I looked down in confusion, "Ah, I see," she continued, "you cannot deny it; well Lucille, I hope soon to convince you that our bill of fare is both wholesome and proper for the pupils, I shall give you one dozen cuts with the rod, and then let you off if you promise not to offend in the same way again."

The nun who was called Serena, now placed a long stool in the middle of the apartment, and made me lie on it full length face downwards, then I felt her cold busy hands as they turned up my clothes, and opened my drawers behind, till my bottom was left naked to the attack of the Lady Superior.

"Do you, Mdlle. Lucille," she asked sternly, "consider that our fare of bread and porridge three times a day, and meat or soup twice a week, added for dinner is only fit for a dog? Ah! Ha!" she went on, cutting me slowly and severely at every few words. "This will give you a better appetite: how do you like the birch sauce, Miss Dainty Mouth?"

I screamed with the pain, and plunged about so that Sister Serena had to hold me down with all her weight upon my shoulders. "Forgive me, oh, forgive me this time, I won't speak to Olive again!" I gasped out as the heavy woman almost stopped my breath, but at last it was over, and after kissing the rod and making me look at the blood-stained weals on my bottom, they sent me away with a caution how I spoke about that or anything else I might see done in the convent.

I longed to have my revenge on the deceitful Olive, but knew not where to turn for a confidant, they all perhaps would be equally treacherous. I stuck to my lessons and avoided punishment as much as possible, being assured that the longer I brooded on my revenge the more complete it would be in the end, at the same I thoroughly studied every part of the building to which I was allowed access, in the hope I might some day find it very useful if I wanted to effect my escape.

The nuns I believe slept in dormitories, where there were a dozen or more to-gether, but every pupil had a very small room to herself, mine was in a long corridor, and Olive's three or four doors from mine, there were neither locks or bolts or any door, as the Lady Superior and elder sisters were supposed to take frequent peeps at us in our sleep; I had at last matured my plan, and having everything in readiness, one dark night when there was not even a glimpse of moonlight, I patiently watched till some of the principals had paid the accustomed visit, and heard the cracked voice of an old nun say, "fast asleep," as I feigned to be in a deep slumber.

Soon their footsteps died away in the corridor, and after waiting sometime, till I felt sure every pupil must be again asleep, if the going round should have awakened them, I crept out of bed, and providing myself with some pins and a strong piece of cord, was soon at the bedside of the treacherous girl I wanted to serve out; my first act was to quietly pass my cord around her, outside the small bed, so that I could suddenly draw it tight and secure her a helpless victim in my power then suddenly stuffing the bedclothes into her mouth before she could scream out, ordered her in a rough whisper to keep quiet or I would kill her; it was too dark to see her terrified face, but she shuddered all over, and seemed as if her very blood was chilled, so cold did she seem to my touch.

Taking advantage of her fright, hands and feet were instantly tied so that she was spread out in a helpless fashion; I made her own handkerchief, which I happened to get hold of, into a gag, and at the same time could feel the drops of cold sweat upon her temples. Now I turned up the bedclothes or pushed them off, as I was tying the cord, till she was quite naked from the bosom downwards.

My hands roved over the soft, firm, naked flesh of her belly, then to the mount of love, which I found just beginning to be fledged with silky down. My fingers sought the crack below, and I could not help amusing myself by frigging her with all my might, the two first fingers of my right hand ruthlessly pushing into her cunny, and I knew caused her intense pain; from the slight groans which the gag could not entirely suppress.

What pleasure it was to me to torture her by my roughness, and outrage her every sense of modesty, although I was too ignorant at the time to know that my fingers were actually taking the poor girl's virginity; a kind of fury possessed me, and I actually bit the lips of her cunny, and munched off as much of the silky down as I could bite away; the pain must have been intense, and her writhing, shuddering agony was so much bliss to me.

At last to finish her off I got a piece of the cord, and passing it right along her crack, tied it round her thighs and waist as tightly and painfully as possible, and then for ornament stuck a lot of pins in the plump cheeks of her bottom and left them there.

My revenge was complete, so wiping my fingers on the bedclothes, for fear of any blood-stains, &c., I left my victim just as she was, to be tormented by her horrible pains and fears till some one might find it out, and release her in the morning.

This outrage was never discovered, my victim was found in-sensible next morning, and remained in a delirious state for three or four weeks before she recovered consciousness, and then the agony and terror she had endured on that awful night had so turned her brain that she believed it was the devil who had so grossly ill-used her, but I heard that one of the father confessors was strongly suspected of having committed the atrocity.

The Superior, with whom Olive had been a favourite, now vented her spite in every direction amongst the young lady pupils of the seminary, and I for one soon fell under her displeasure, and was ordered to be tied up to their whipping post; it was only for slightly oversleeping myself, and not dressing quickly when the bell rang for us to get up at 6. A. M.

I was suspended by my wrists being tied high up the post as I stood upon a small footstool, then it was suddenly kicked away, the jerk of the sudden strain on my wrists almost making the straps cut into the flesh. My feet were dangling some inches from the ground. "Oh! Oh! Ah—r—r—r—re!" I screamed. "How cruel! Oh! Papa! Papa! If only you knew how they were treating me in this awful place!"

Lady Superior (who seemed delighted at the sight of my pain).—"Hold your foolish noise, Mdlle. Lucille, wait till you have something to scream about, girl." Then the old Serena, who it seemed was always in attendance at punishment time, pinned up my skirts and opened my drawers behind, and the Superior went on, "This rod shall make all the sluggards turn out quicker in the morning; what do you think, Mademoiselle, of making us all wait prayers for ten minutes? Will you wake—wake—wake up sharper in future?"

She gave me three smarting cuts at each word, and my suspended position added so much to the intensity of my pain, that I screamed, kicked, and plunged about as I swung by my wrists from the post. "Sister Serena," exclaimed the Superior, "keep the girl steady or I cannot plant my cuts as effectually as I ought to do upon her naughty impudent bottom, she shan't sleep for a week if I can only make it sore enough!" Serena now held me to the post with one hand, to prevent my swaying about, whilst the rod rained a succession of withering, scorching cuts on my buttocks, and just underneath the parting of the cheeks of my bottom. My screams were heartrending, but they only seemed to enjoy it more and the Superior never ended her objurgations till the rod was worn out.

Things now went on till I was nearly fourteen, we never had a holiday, and only short letters came to me from home, in which my father constantly expressed his hopes of my improvement, and seemed quite oblivious to all I had written from time to time about my severe treatment, and begging him to remove me to some other school.

I afterwards found out that my home letters were regularly suppressed, and others more suitable were written and sent to papa, in my name; what a wretch that Superior now appears in my eyes, she not only delighted in whipping us nearly to death, but forged letters to our parents so as to keep her pupils, and make everything appear *couleur de rose*.

Perhaps, dear Rosa, you have heard that I managed to escape from that dreadful convent, but previous to that they nearly killed me. I was getting quite a big girl, my pussey already sported its silken down on the Mons. Veneris, which we all consider such an ornament to our secret charms.

The Superior had lately taken much notice of me, and introduced me to a clique of her favourites, three or four pretty girls about my own age, who were often indulged with little treats in her private room; there, we girls were encouraged and instructed in all kinds of lascivious ideas; we looked at each other's cunnies, tickled and kissed each other in every possible way, the Superior encouraging us, and suggesting a variety of attitudes for us to try. She had a huge godemiche, about nine inches long, and very thick, which she would fit upon one of the girls, and then submit herself to be fucked as hard as possible, whilst the other girls had to turn up the girl's skirts, and smack her bottom hard and fast, with the palms of their hands, to make the young gentleman (as the Superior called her partner) work fast and vigorously.

Then she would have us all strip naked, whilst we had in turn to kiss and suck her cunt, when it was all slimy with her spendings.

I did not mind the slapping, or allowing any one to kiss and tongue-fuck my cunny, but the Superior's was so hairy, and had such meaty looking lips, and a huge clitoris, (which I now know is induced by long-continued self-abuse), and it smelt so fishy, that I absolutely declined the honour of gamahuching her, and nothing could induce me to do so.

This so enraged her that she flew at me like a tigress. I was knocked down, and beaten with a thick stick, till my flesh was bruised all over, and then picked up, almost fainting, and hurried off to my own little room.

Perhaps nothing further would have happened, but in my innocence, I supposed my letters were sent home just as I sealed them up, so I wrote to Miss Birch a full account of what I had been seduced into, and the dreadful beating I had received, for not liking the cunt of the Lady Superior.

The very next day after I thought the letter was gone, the old nun, Serena, fetched me into a dull gloomy room, which I had never been in before, but at once rightly judged to be a punishment chamber, where I saw a high whipping post, made of a square beam, set upright in the floor, with two rings near the top on each side, by which to tie up the victim; a birch rod was hanging on the wall, and two scourges with long thongs lay upon a seat at one end, but I had no time for further observation, as the Superior seemed to follow us into the room almost immediately.

"Now, Mdlle. Lucille," she exclaimed, grinding her teeth in rage, "you shall rue the insult you put upon me the other day, before my special favourites, of which I had minded to make you one, so that when you left the seminary you might look back with pleasure to the loving amusements I had first introduced you to; perhaps I should have overlooked it all, but see I have your letter. Ha! Ha!! you little fool to think that would ever go out of the convent!"

Sister Serena had by this time put me on a stool, and was fastening my wrists one on each side of the post, and presently the stool was removed, and I found myself just touching the floor with the tips of my toes.

"What a beautiful position, how she will twist about and scream when she feels the scourge, make haste to bare her bottom, as I am burning to pay her out. Ha! Ha!! Mdlle. Lucille, I fancy you wouldn't mind kissing my cunt now if I promised to let you off," said the Superior spitefully.

My courage and natural obstinacy came to my assistance at the moment, I was so indignant, and the idea was so repulsive to me that I resolved rather to die than do that for her; I was frightened and yet flushed with shame and indignation at my treatment, besides something seemed to advise me to irritate my tormentor to do her worst, and get it over quickly.

"No! No!! No, never!!! you may kill me, and then I should be out of my misery!" I exclaimed.

She scowled with ferocity, but said with all the calmness she could command, "make haste, Serena, up with her clothes, and open the drawers well, and keep her as steady as possible." Then taking up the instrument of punishment I could see it consisted of five or six long thongs of whipcord, plaited and knotted at the ends, fixed on a very elastic handle.

It was poised in her hand for a moment, and then brought down with stinging force on my exposed buttocks, then again, and again, and again, in quick succession; each cut seemed to sear the flesh as if done by a red hot iron, my piercing screams filled the whole place, and the Superior, her eyes sparkling with ferocious joy jeered me about how I liked the scourge. "How lovely you look, Mdlle. Lucille, as you plunge and scream, and I know the intense agony of every cut; would you rather die now, my little dear? Well, I've a good mind to kill you, outright, only I want to keep you as long as that *dear, kind papa* of yours is willing to pay! How he must have loved his Lucille, to place her with me; I'm so kind, so very kind, you know, my dear girl! What do you think of my kindness, you little love?"

Her cuts were awful, and I swayed and plunged so that it was impossible for Serena to keep my body steady, so she seized the other scourge, and tried her best to second the Superior in her efforts to cut me up more and more.

At last they fairly panted for breath, as I was left dangling, sobbing and moaning, with my clothes torn, my drawers in shreds, and streaming with blood all down my thighs and legs.

Fearing I might faint, they poured a little strong cordial down my parched throat, sponged my face with cold water, and put some strong snuff up my nose, which almost drove me into convulsions, so very violent was the fit of sneezing produced.

28

They seemed carried away with delight at the sight of my sufferings, and sprinkled a quantity of the snuff over the cuts on my bottom, just to dry up the blood, as they said with a laugh. Next all my clothes were cut or torn off, till I had nothing on but slippers, stockings, and the remains of my drawers.

"Now we'll finish off the obstinate, impudent little beast, I wish I dare kill her," said the Superior, grinding her teeth, "only I should lose too much, she is worth more alive than dead."

A couple of lady's riding whips were now produced, and the two women attacked me afresh; I was cut all over my body, each cut seemed as if done with a red hot knife, the blood flowed down my back in streams, and yet their rage seemed to increase at the sight of my sufferings. My screams were awful, but only so much music to their ears. They jeered and derided my cries for "God to have mercy on me, &c.," said "my time was come to die, but they would make me last as long as possible, and draw out my agony to the very last gasp."

This must all have passed in a very short time, but was an age of intense suffering to me, and the finale was such a display of ferocity that I sank under it, and thus robbed them of the pleasure of prolonging my torture. The Superior seized me by the hair, and drawing my head back, lashed her whip across my face and bosom, drawing more blood at every cut, whilst old Serena, not to be outdone, took my right leg under her arm, cut me dreadfully inside my thighs, along the crack of my pussey, and made the tip of her whip reach the Mons. Veneris.

This was the last I could recollect, but when I came to myself I was in my own bed, wrapped up in cloths soaked in water. No bones were broken, and my health soon recovered sufficiently to enable me to effect my escape, and avoid their further malice.

CHAPTER III.

Lucille's Marriage and Adventures.

It was about 3 A.M. one fine morning when I escaped from the Ursuline Convent, and made my way to the Hotel d'Angleterre; the porter in answer to my summons was about to refuse to give me refuge, when a young Englishman, who was just taking his candle in the hall, said, "He'd be damned if I should not be taken care of," and ordered the chambermaid to be called to attend on me, and added that he would be responsible for all expenses. "Certainly, my lord," said the porter of the hotel, but he added *sotto voce*, "I think he's a fool to be so easily imposed upon."

I was too glad to have found a protector, (especially when I found he was an aristocrat), so I quietly followed the *femme de chambre*, and was content to await awhile for the *denouement* of my adventure.

Breakfast was brought to me about eleven o'clock, and also a message to say that Lord Dunwich, would do himself the pleasure of waiting upon me in an hour's time.

You may be sure I was all impatience to see the kind fellow who had stood my friend, and was most agreeably surprised to find his manners quite equal to his appearance when I saw him again.

His Lordship was greatly interested by the account of my

escape from the convent, and said he was a very particular friend of my betrothed husband, the Earl of Ellington, and would put me under the protection of a lady going to England, who would see me safe home. He was such a handsome fellow, and my gratitude was so gushing that at the moment I could have refused him no thing and was delighted by the way he lingered over a kiss, he would insist upon as his due, my whole soul seemed to leap towards the generous fellow, and tears of disappointment stood in my eyes when he was gone.

I never saw him again till my wedding day, two years later, when he was best man to my husband, and in my eyes looked a thousand times more loveable.

A married couple of sixteen and twenty-eight ought to have been blessed with every happiness, but soon after the first three days of our honeymoon the Earl's temper seemed so overbearing and imperious, that I began seriously to regret my fate, and looked forward to a life of gilded misery. The Earl was fond of the turf, and often left me alone whilst he spent a fortnight at Newmarket or Doncaster and York.

One day I was agreeably surprised by a call from Lord Dunwich, (we were living in Grosvenor Square at the time), he looked more handsome than ever, and seemed so full of sympathy for me in every respect that I could not help falling into tears, and telling him all my fears, and how I was neglected for nasty ugly four-legged brutes of race-horses, and that in fact I was sure Lord Ellington loved his Derby favourite better than myself, and would rather I broke my neck than his pet should fall lame.

"Ah, Lucille," he said, falling on his knees before me, "how your distress cuts me to the quick, would to God I could comfort you in any way! I have loved you from the first moment we met, although I knew you belonged to a bosom friend, and now the wretch slights you; look up, dear Lucille, from your tears, smile upon one who is devoted to you body and soul!" And then seizing my hand, upon which he imprinted a lot of impassioned kisses, "Ah, you will pardon my presumptuous love, how can I help it?"

I was piqued by the Earl's coldness towards me, and something impelled me to pity the handsome suitor at my feet, so that although the tears were still welting from my eyes, could not help smiling and caressing his head as he looked up to my face.

"Darling Lucille, I may call you so now, you respond to my love, my happiness is too great," he exclaimed, drawing my unresisting body down, so that our lips quickly met in a rapturous kiss of real love.

I was lost, and he so rapidly took advantage of everything, that proceeding from one liberty to another, in less than ten minutes I was an adultress, but what a sweet sin, what transports of love shot through our souls as we melted away again and again in the extasies of mutual enjoyment; how we toyed with each other's most secret charms, and promised to renew our forbidden pleasure at every convenient opportunity.

Alas, for our happiness, some spy informed the Earl of my sweet *liaison*, he made an excuse to visit Brussels with me and again I found myself incarcerated in a hateful convent.

The kindness of my husband on our journey from England (which I afterwards found was only a part of his most artful programme), had so imposed upon my rather soft-hearted nature, that I really felt sorry that I had ever been unfaithful to my marriage vows, although no doubt the image of my loving paramour was firmly imprinted in my heart.

We went to operas, bal masques, saw all the sights, and enjoyed ourselves immensely for a few days and being strict Catholics he one day said jestingly, "I suppose, Lucille, we must go to confession, and get absolution after having enjoyed ourselves, and confess all the delightful sins we have committed; by-the-bye, be sure you do not forget to confess having ridden a St. George on your husband, and allowed him to spend his seed in your hand, or on your pretty bosom, they are most awful sins, and will cost a pretty penny for absolution. I should not be surprised if the Rev. Father undertook to inflict personal chastisement *à la Girard et Cadière*," he added, laughing.

"But, seriously," I answered, "apart from joking, I know we ought to do it, and will go to that church in the Rue de la

Madeleine this very day, I know I am a sinner, but don't like to make a laugh of such serious things."

Then seating myself on his knee, I drew his face to mine, and kissed him lovingly, as I added, "But, dear Francis, you won't leave your little wife so long again, will you, for those horrid horses? You can't imagine how dull and low spirited I get when left all by myself."

"What a pretty pouting little bride you look. Why, Lucille, the way you kiss excites me as if we were still on the honeymoon trip; but dearest," he added, "a sporting man must see his horses tried and run, then, you know, I shall make up in the winter what you lose in the summer; there's nothing else to do then but to make love. Ha, you sweet little devil, do you want to commit another sin before confession?"

My hand had been gently caressing his prick outside his breeches, till it was now rampant and impatient of the restraining cloth.

"Well," he went on, following my example, by passing a hand up my clothes, and gently tickling my clitoris with his forefinger, "we'll lump it all together, so there won't be any more to pay. My Stars, Lucille, how excitable you are. You're spending on my fingers. It's nothing to blush about, little simpleton."

I got off his lap, and kneeling before him, unbuttoned his flap, and the engine of love seemed to leap into my hand, its fiery head, with the skin turned back, looked so tempting, that I could not resist the temptation to kiss and caress it for a few minutes. My tongue played lasciviously round the tender and excitable surface, whilst my hands were fondling his finely developed balls.

"Darling! Darling!" he ejaculated. "It's coming! Oh! I can't stop—kiss—kiss—suck it. Take it in your mouth, Lucille! Oh! Ah! How delicious! You darling, to think you would give me so much pleasure!"

I was as excited as himself and sucked and swallowed his delicious spendings to the very last drop, as he pressed my head down with his hands, and gasped out his hands, and gasped out his ejaculations of extasy.

"Now, it's my turn, Sir. I mean to have a St. George, as you lie on the hearthrug. Come, down with you at once, or I will bite it off," making him feel my teeth, as I playfully took it again in my mouth.

We had a delightful bout on the hearthrug, and I rode him till he spent into my excited cunt a third time. Keeping his cock stiff, and starting him again after each spend by the contractions of the folds of my vagina, which he declared gave him the most exquisite and voluptuous sensations, and that he had never experienced anything to equal it in his life many women as he had in his time.

Presently I told him that as soon as I could get dressed I would go to confession.

"Do love," he replied, "and if the Confessor is reasonable with you, I will go myself to-morrow, or send for him to wait on me at the hotel."

I left him smoking a cigar, and about an hour-and-a-half afterwards entered the church, where I was immediately accosted by an elderly priest. "If the English lady wishes to confess, the Father Francisco in yonder box is most suitable for Madame. He knows the English ways so well, and was consecrated in England."

I approached the box, which was in a very secluded corner of the sacred building, and kneeling on a hassock, enquired, in a low voice, "If the Rev. Father Francisco was ready to hear my confession?"

"Yes, my daughter, and I pray God you may have nothing but venial sins to confess," was the reply of my unseen Confessor.

In my innocence I related every act of our married life: how excited we were in our love games, and the various attitudes we used to heighten our enjoyment.

"Awfully sensual, my daughter. Your Confessor previous to marriage must have admonished you as to the use of these unnatural postures in following the dictates of nature in your endeavours to obey the first commandment, 'to increase and multiply'. The holy rite of matrimony ought not to be perverted by lascivious ideas and filthy sacrifices to lust. It is a most serious thing my daughter, but before I consider what penance to exact for such sins, tell me, as you value the intercession of our Holy Mother, have you always been faithful to your husband? If only by a look or gesture, it is important to your salvation hereafter that you should confess it now."

I was silent, dumbfounded for a moment or two. "Ah! my daughter, conceal nothing. Alas! it is as I feared—conceal nothing from me, or it will be impossible for me to grant you absolution."

Thus pressed, and feeling but a full confession would avail me with the Confessor, I told him everything, and especially how sorry I felt at having allowed my pique at the Earl's neglect to have carried me into such a *liaison,* and that the tender regard he had lately exhibited towards me smote me to the quick for my unfaithfulness, and that that was the reason I had so given way to lasciviousness with him, in order to compensate, by the perfect abandon of my love, for any suspicions he might entertain.

"My daughter, I must consult our Superior. Yours is such a serious case, and I beg that you will go into the vestry, by the door behind this box, and wait a few minutes, till I bring you his decision," said Father Francisco.

I was all of a tremble, my face felt hot with blushes of shame and I longed to hide from observation for a few minutes, so I readily went into the vestry, as he had requested. It was a bare scantily furnished room, with a few chairs, a writing table covered with papers, and some priests' frocks and vestments hanging round the walls.

Presently the old priest who had accosted me on my first entering the church, came to conduct me to Father Francisco's room, but instead of that, I found myself in the cell of a convent, with the door locked behind me.

The worst fears assailed my frightened mind; I sank on my knees, calling on God and my husband to release me, crying and stamping in impotent rage by turns; this must have lasted an hour or two. Then a little wicket was opened in the door, and the same old priest told me to calm myself, for Father Francisco and the Superior were praying to the Holy Mother to direct them what penance to impose upon such a sinner, and that I must remain where I was till next day, when, he added, "no doubt you will be restored to your loving husband, as pure in mind and spirit as when you first took your marriage vows."

I was going to implore him to allay the Earl's anxiety on my behalf, but he assured me they had sent to his lordship to say that I was doing penance for some hours in their convent, and quickly closed the *guichet*, so that I was again left alone.

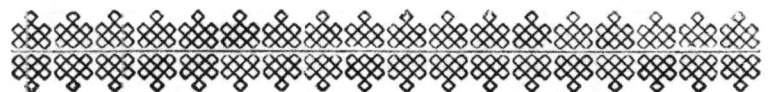

CHAPTER IV.

The Penance

Two nuns supplied me with refreshment, made me up a bed on the floor, and I really had nothing to complain of as to treatment that first night, still, something seem to assure me that I really was a prisoner, and should not so easily get out of the convent. My hope was, that the Earl would speedily insist upon my speedy release, (little dreaming at the moment that he was the instigator of my detention, and had actually acted as confessor in the assumed name of Father Francisco.)

My anxiety was greatly increased the next day, when hour after hour passed, and still no communication from the Confessor or Superior, the nuns who brought me in breakfast and dinner were silent to all my enquiries or offers of bribes if they would help me get out of the place.

My watch stopped for want of a key, but about seven o'clock in the evening as near as I could guess, the old priest opened the door, and beckoned me to follow him. My heart suddenly recovered its courage, and I braced up my nerves to bear the severest penance; we passed along several passages, and at last opening a door, he motioned me to enter. There, sitting before a small table, which had a bible and crucifix upon it, sat a rather young priest, about the same age as my husband, but with a close shaven face and crown (the Earl had heavy whiskers and moustache, I had never seen him otherwise), and he struck me as being like Francis about the nose and eyes, still, no suspicion that it could really be him came into my mind.

"Daughter Lucille, Lady Ellington," said the seated Confessor, as the other locked the door behind me. "In answer to prayer, the Holy Mother has inspired us to grant you absolution, only after the most severe personal chastisement and humiliations we can possibly inflict upon you. Then, you will return to your confiding loving husband, purified of your adulterous sins, but for all that, he will still, and for the rest of his life, wear the horns of a cuckolded husband, which is his punishment for teaching you such lascivious ideas; it is an awful sin to so abandon yourselves to lust, and your unfaithfulness is the providential punishment he so well deserves."

My face and neck were suffused with the blushes of burning shame, as my eyes fell beneath his ardent gaze, besides something instinctively told me that both Father Francisco and his coadjutor were enjoying the sight of my confusion.

"Now please divest yourself of everything you have on, except corset, chemise and drawers, whilst I prepare this scourger for the chastisement of your wicked sensual flesh, and my brother here will get that rope in order, ready to tie up your hands above your head."

I scarcely knew how I got my dress and skirts off, as my hands trembled so, and the idea of stripping before two men, even if they were priests, was so distressing to my sense of modesty, but, somehow or other, I was soon standing up, with my skirts on the floor, about my heels, and my last under petticoat tucked up under my corset.

Father Francisco confronted me, scourge in hand, and pointing with his finger to my drawers in front, roughly ordered me to open them, and show where I had admitted my lover, when in the act of committing adultery. "Open it, you wicked woman. I must see the seat of lust itself!"

He flourished his scourge so, and gave me two such terrible cuts round my buttocks, that I was compelled to obey his immodest and shameful order, and the moment I had done so, he produced a pair of scissors and denuded me of nearly all the dark, silky chevelure I took such delight in viewing in the glass, when ever I cressed myself, or just got out of my morning bath.

"I suppose you were so excited and wanton, when Lord Dunwich embraced you, that you shewed him everything, even your nakedness, as the Bible calls it; did you blush then, as you pretend to do now, Lucille?" he asked.

My surprise and indignation almost choked me, so that I was unable to speak, and he gave me a heavy slap with his hand on my bottom, saying, "So you will not answer, and think I am behaving shamefully, do you? It's nothing to what you will have to submit to presently, Lady Ellington; turn round and open your legs, and stoop forward this instant, or I will flog the very life out of you!"

His rude hand was passed under my bottom, between my legs, and as I covered my face with my hands, I could feel his fingers invade every secret spot in turn, even to forcing a digit up the fundamental orifice, which is always so tight and difficult of entrance, saying, as he did so: "Did you let him go there, or has your husband ever sodomised your bum-hole? Ha! Ha! How modest we are now. Speak: say if you ever allowed any one to put his prick in your arse?"

I cannot recollect all he said or questioned me about, but his words and actions were every moment more and more coarse and obscene, on purpose to add to my humiliation.

"Here, Father Anthony," he continued, addressing the old priest, "where is your godemiche? That's the thing to draw all the wantonness out of her lustful body. It is well furnished with good stiff bristles?"

FATHER ANTHONY.—"It's a new one, same as we always keep in stock to subdue the fleshly lusts of these lascivious female sinners, and never used before, but I must tie her up."

The rope, which hung from a pulley in the ceiling, was tied tightly round my wrists, bringing both hands together; then he pulled it as hard as possible till I could barely touch the floor with my feet, and all my weight was upon my arms and the muscles of my back.

"That's it, exactly," chuckled Francisco. "Now, my dear Lucille, Lady Ellington I ought to say, you will really enjoy the insertion of this jolly dildoe up your cunt, and it is full of a delightful injection, with which it will spend in response to your emission of pleasure."

"Ah! No! No! Oh pray don't treat me with such brutality," I screamed, in horror, when I saw the huge red-headed thing, with its shaft springing from a bed of bristles, fixed round the balls so as to prick the cunt at every insertion, besides its length and thickness seemed quite terrible to contemplate. "I am quite content to submit to your penance of scourging and whipping, but oh, oh, have mercy, and put that thing out of my sight."

FATHER FRANCISCO.—"Look, you need not be so frightened. I shall lubricate it well with perfumed oil to make it enter easily, besides I will put some on your cunt and bottom." Suiting his actions to his word, and oiling my privates profusely, especially my bottom-hole, which he lubricated till he could easily work two fingers in at once.

It was dreadfully disgusting, but still his frigging my bottom was rather exciting, and he could tell or guess my feelings, as he went on to say, "I see you like it, but the dildoe will make you plunge and spend with delight."

He then took up my legs; one under each arm, and stood between them, so they were wide apart, and Father Anthony, his face plainly showing how he delighted in the task, proceeded to force his godemiche into me, opening the lips of my cunt with his fingers till the head was fairly in, then ruthlessly shove, shove, shove, till, "Ah! Ah! Oh! Ah—r—r—r—re!" I screamed in dreadful pain, as the sharp bristles ran into the tender surroundings of my pussey. "Ah! Ah! Oh, my God!" I screamed plunging and writhing in my agony, his eyes glared into mine with a fiendish delight, only equalled by the look of his companion, who held my legs like a vice, and encouraged him to fuck the wanton woman till she had had enough to keep her out adultery for a long time to come.

Presently Father Francisco, digging his nails into the flesh of my legs, said excitedly, "See, see, she's coming. The gluey spend is glistening on your dildoe. Now, now, shoot it into her; let her enjoy it!"

In a moment I felt the hot gush of the contents of the godemiche. It rather relieved me for a moment or two, but oh, oh, my dear, even after this long lapse of time, I can never forget the agony of that moment. The whole of my body seemed filled with liquid fire, for they had filled the dildoe with some infernal decoction on purpose to ruin my health, and destroy all chance of my ever enjoying the sweets of love again. Such I know was their intent, for they taunted me with it at the time; but although I never quite recovered from the shock to my system, and feel even now that it was the original cause of my premature decay, they did not succeed in depriving me of all sensual desire or feelings for the future.

I fainted, but they never let me down, and when at last I began to recover consciousness Father Francisco was using his scourge most unmercifully on my buttocks, the drawers being open, and the naked flesh exposed to every cut.

"I thought this would bring her round," exclaimed he. "See, Father Anthony, her eyes are opening, it will soon make her forget the dildoe fucking, she did enjoy that, did she not, Anthony? But she'll be a long time before she has such pleasure again. Ha! Ha! Ha!!! how lovely she is getting, see her wriggle from the pain of every cut. Ah, Lucille, dear Lady Ellington, what intense delight the sight of your agony is to us."

By this time either he was tired, or he thought a little respite would enable me to bear more presently, so dropping the scourge on the floor he left me still suspended, whilst himself and assistant sat down and gloated over the sight of my suspended figure and blood-stained bottom, with their hands under their frocks, and I verily believe now they were frigging themselves.

After about ten minutes Father Francisco again approached,

scourge in hand, whilst the elder priest gave me a few drops of cordial, and held some pungent salts under my nose to refresh me a little. "That will do," said the former, "stand back, Father Anthony. Now, now, you wicked, wanton, lustful young woman, did you wish your husband dead when having connexion with Lord Dunwich? Why don't you answer? Were his parts more pleasing to your sensuality? Is he better furnished than your husband? Speak up; confess all your wickedness! Did no sense of shame shock you in the midst of your enjoyment with that fellow, eh?"

Every question brought a scathing cut with it, breaking the weals and drawing fresh blood at every stroke, but I really was so ashamed I knew not how to answer, and my tongue was useless except for moans or cries of pain, and notwithstanding all their degrading and cruel treatment I felt it was fully deserved by me.

"Won't you speak? won't you confess your sorrow for your sin?" he continued. "Are you really so lost to all sense of shame as to be hardened against repentance? This must be whipped, yes, whipped out of you, even if it nearly costs your life!"

Just then Father Anthony loosed the rope a little, so that I could shrink further from the blows of the scourge, till I was driven up to the wall, where I stood on tiptoe with my hands drawn up over my head, and my back bending as much as possible to avoid the terrible shower of blows with which he was cutting up my buttocks still more and more.

Crimson with shame, tears flowing in torrents from my starting eyes, I moaned, cried and implored for mercy, protesting in a broken voice, "That ever since my husband had renewed his kindness to me I had been very, very sad and ashamed of myself for what I had done, and only his former neglect had caused me to throw myself into the arms of a handsome man to whom I was under great obligations for protecting me when I escaped from the Ursuline Convent."

"Ha, then, you are that Lucille who insulted Lady Superior, I heard all about it at the time!" he went on furiously. "Now you shall be punished for that too," seizing my left leg and lifting it up, so that he could cut freely under my thighs, on my sore cunny, and every tenderest spot he could think of, whilst old Father Anthony was rubbing his hands in delight at the sight.

My agony was so intense that I could only gasp and sigh, strength I had none, he seemed beside himself with rage, but at last dropped his scourge, and throwing open his frock in front I could feel his rampant pego thrusting towards my mount, and am sure he spent on my drawers outside before he could get into me; this he soon effected, and taking my buttocks up in his strong embrace, he fucked furiously, swaying me about with my arms still tied up by the rope; but I forgot all that, his motions within me took away all feeling of pain, and I believe much as I loathed him and felt humiliated by all his dreadful treatment that I actually spent copiously when I felt his hot sperm shooting into and soothing my overheated cunt.

He was so overcome that Father Anthony seeing he was about to fall, released me, or loosened the rope so that we sank down together on the floor, and laid almost motionless for a few minutes, till the old priest, taking up a scourge, began to whip us both unmercifully, and made Francisco get up. This was the end for that time, but I was ordered to prepare for a final penance in a day or two's time.

CHAPTER V.

The Last Scène and Denouement.

They kept me in the same chamber, where I had been so outraged, the two nuns nursing,—bathing my bruises, and using soothing injections to allay the inflammations of my privates, till, on the third day, they said I was so far recovered that my Confessors might finish the prescribed penance, adding, with a malicious smile, "we saw everything last time, and so we shall now, through our peepholes; how delicious the sight was last time, and we had such frigging and dildoe fucks after it was all over."

Having said this, they speedily disappeared and I was left to await my fate in trembling anxiety; I was hot and cold by turns, as the recollection of all the humiliating and painful incidents of the other day came back so vividly to my mind, and in imagination I seemed to suffer all my tortures over again.

This did not last long, although you may be sure it seemed long enough to me in my state of apprehension. A key was turned in the lock, and the door creaked on its hinges: my persecuting confessors again stood before me in reality, with quite a sardonic expression of anticipated pleasure on their faces; no trace of pity could I find on either visage, nothing but gloating sensuality seemed to animate the ardent looks with which they regarded me for some moments.

The hateful Francisco was the first to address me, a smile of terrible meaning playing round his mouth, showing his pearly white teeth to such perfection that I was again strongly reminded of my husband.

"Lady Ellington, I hope, has had good time for reflection upon the heinousness of her sins, particularly those in contravention of her marriage vows; wantonness is as nothing compared to that. What has the penitent Lucille to say? Has her chastisement made her feel the pangs of real remorse?" he said, whisking a scourge before my face.

I was too frightened to speak; face, neck and bosom, I could feel, were in a burning heat, whilst me eyes could not meet his, for something more than shame instinctively told me what I might have to suffer at his hands.

"No sign of repentance here, Father Anthony; she must be stripped naked at once. Do you hear, Lucille? Strip—strip—strip at once, or it will be much the worse for you!" he said with rough ferocity.

Both priests helped me to undress, and in their impetuous haste almost tore the clothes off my back, at the same time taking all sorts of disgusting liberties, and keeping me in a continued state of confusion, at last when nothing was left but my chemise to remove, they suddenly tied the rope round my left ancle, and in an instant I found myself suspended head downwards, with the right leg kicking in the air, and screaming piteously for mercy.

"Secure her wrists to the rings in the floor," said Francisco, "and then help me to whip the seat of lust till she is a little more repentant."

The elder priest speedily effected this, and then both of them with scourges commenced to whip me most mercilessly, aiming their relentless cuts between my legs so as to cut the lips of my cunt and round my bottom-hole at every blow; now and then the cruel thongs would wind round the upper part of my thighs, or on to my mount; my cries were heartrending, as each blow seemed to reopen all my old cuts and bruises. "Ah! Ah—r—r—re! Oh! Oh!! will you never have pity, and believe me sorry for my faults?" I screamed or moaned, and gasped out the words in intense agony.

"So you begin to repent a little under the lash, do you, Lucille, are you really sorry for having wronged Lord Ellington, is it your mind or your cunt that is most filled with remorse? How you seem to writhe, and how prettily we are making it look for you, the trickling blood is delightful to see as it flows in drops and rills over your back and belly!" His questions were spoken slowly as he seemed to enjoy the pleasure of my intense suffering, and two or three of his cuts were over the tender surface of my belly or right across the navel.

"Scream away, you sensual woman, why don't you implore the Holy Virgin to have pity and forgive you, we are only carrying out her commands, are we not Father Francisco?" hissed out old Anthony, as he continued to scourge my back and sides, and every now and then aimed a fearful blow right down my lacerated cunny. Again they would stop for a little, and ask me jeeringly, "about my feeling remorse, would I indulge in such obscenity with my husband again, or keep from adultery in future?"

I was almost too far gone to do more than moan, and Father Anthony suggested that I ought to be well lashed over my neck, shoulders, and bosom, to make me speak out, but the other seeing how exhausted I really was, restrained his mad fury, and then after waiting a little one of them would give me a terrible cut, and ask the other to see the beautiful effects of it as I swayed about in agony; this was done again and again, till after a time the scourges were thrown aside, and the rope being lowered I was allowed to lay on the floor for a little while, and some cordial was again administered to refresh me, my tormentors sitting down and frigging themselves openly before my face, till in the act of spending they would stand over me so that I might be thoroughly humiliated by having all their spendings drop on my face, neck, or head, as I was still secured to the floor by my wrists.

Presently, at a sign from Francisco, his companion hoisted me up by the ancle again, and did it so tightly that I was frightfully stretched by my arms and leg; which were drawn as painfully tight as he could make it, the fastenings cutting into the flesh so that I bear the marks to this very day. I could see that Francisco was again preparing his godemiche with oil, but he did not put any upon my person.

Horrified at this sight, I begged and implored them in the most piteous manner not to degrade me again with that disgusting instrument, promising to pay the Church any amount for absolution rather than endure it again.

"Too late, too late, your repentance is not sincere, besides, the other day we saw with our eyes how your lascivious nature responded to the thrusts of this thing in your cunt, now I am going to degrade your bottom-hole by inserting it there, however painful the operation may prove," saying which he seized, and held my left leg under his arm, and standing close to my body at once proceeded to carry out his infernal idea of ravishing my anus. Lacerated, bleeding, and sore as my bottom was at the least touch, and regardless of my piercing shrieks, he forced the oily head of the india rubber thing quite into my tightly contracted bum-hole, the pain was intense, as it seemed to rend the lining tissue of the anal canal in its passage, and the bristles round its root added, if possible, still more to the intensity of my suffering.

I believe, that giving one long shriek of agony, I lost consciousness for a time, but only to awake and find them laughing and jeering at my sufferings, as the one worked his dildoe in my bottom, whilst the other had thrust two or three fingers up my blood-stained and wounded cunt. It is quite indescribable what I felt at this outrage, the accumulation of shame, agony and horror so overpowered my exhausted nature, that I went off again into such a death-like swoon, that they really feared I was dead, and made haste to let me down as well as apply strong restoratives.

My hands were still retained in the rings on the floor, and the godemiche was left sticking in my bottom, the spasmodic contractions of the sphincter muscle holding it as in a vice, whilst the pulsations of the violated passage behind were still fully as painful. All this was apparent to me as I slowly came to myself once more, and could see the excited looks of my cruel Confessors, who proceeded to sprinkle me with cold water, and use a large sponge for the purpose of both refreshing me and allowing them to gloat over the extent of my hurts.

This lasted a little while, then I was made to get up on my hands and knees, facing Francisco, who then opened his frock, so as to show me the excited state of his prick, at the same time, with a malicious look of fiendish joy, he asked me, "If I should not like to suck such a delightful sweetmeat?" Then seeing my look of intense disgust, he burst into a rage, saying, "Oh! So you mean to insult me as you did the Lady Superior of the Ursulines, do you, Lucille? You may think I am disgusting and nasty, or I smell strong as she did, and I may tell you, to make you relish it still more, that scarcely an hour ago it was up the strong smelling cunt of that very same lady, and I was careful not to wash, so that you might have the full benefit of the delicious aroma of her spendings."

Speechless with disgust, and helpless in every way, it was useless for me to appeal for mercy or consideration from two such heartless beings; the only thing I could do was to close my eyes to the awful sight.

But only for a moment, a tremendous whack from Father Anthony, who had taken up the scourge, made me shriek out again, "Ah! Ah! Oh! Will you never finish me off, and kill me in mercy?" The only answer I had was a quick repetition of the blow, whilst the repulsive Francisco's right hand, clutching my hair, pulled my head up, and drew it back so painfully, that I gasped for breath. This was exactly what he wanted, and, in a moment, his prick was forced into my mouth. The sensation was so repulsive, horrible, and choking all at once, that I had not the presence of mind to bite, or he would have repented the act ever after. Old Anthony was cutting my back, bottom, thighs, and loins, even the calves of my legs not escaping his frenzied scourging. Blood was streaming over my flesh, and dripping to the floor in little pools, and I felt I was really dying at last. Just then the excited Francisco shot a deluge of hot sperm into my mouth and throat;

I was choked, and remember no more, except, that on recovering consciousness, the supposed Confessor, Francisco, was dressed as a gentleman, and I immediately recognised him as my husband, as, at the same instant, he exclaimed, "Woman, my revenge is complete. You won't deceive me again. How I have revelled in degrading, humiliating, and torturing my adulterous wife. You'll never see me more. This has been my way of divorcing myself from a faithless bitch."

He was gone before I could find words to reply, but my sense of pain was instantly drowned in a deep desire for vengeance for this outrage, and its impulse so strengthened me, that I was soon well enough to travel.

My lover, Lord Dunwich, received me with open arms, and declared he would shoot or be shot by the Earl ere forty-eight hours had elapsed; at once despatching a friend with his cartel to arrange a meeting for the next morning in Hyde Park at the dawn of day.

We spent the night together at his hotel, although scarcely fourteen days since I was so fearfully outraged, how we fucked all night, and swam in sensual pleasures for hours, I would deny him nothing, was he not my champion, who was going to risk his life in the morning to avenge my fearful wrongs, and to make him still more earnest in his desire for vengeance, I stripped naked, let him examine every part, where the marks of the bruises and lacerations were still visible; my cunt he sucked, kissed and fucked till I was beside myself with excitement, and he was also ready for anything, then my poor bum-hole attracted his attention, he kissed and put his tongue into it, till I was eager to have him there, and begged he would put his prick in gently at first for fear of hurting me too much; this was a heavenly finish to our night of love; we swam in delight, never before or since have I tasted voluptuous joy to equal that *enculade*.

Next morning dressed as a young gentleman with a false moustache, I went as one of his seconds to the fatal place of meeting, and had the satisfaction of seeing my wrongs avenged by a ball through the heart of my hated husband. We then went abroad for a while, but my dear lover lost his life by drowning in the Rhine, since which I have consoled myself as you know by all sorts of erotic fancies, especially flagellation, and now my dear Rosa at the early age of twenty-five I find myself fast fading away.

FINIS.

MISS COOTE'S
CONFESSION

Miss Coote's

Confession,

OR

THE VOLUPTUOUS EXPERIENCES

OF AN OLD MAID

> Some have been beaten till they know
> What wood a cudgel's of by th' blow ;
> Some kick'd, until they can feel whether
> A shoe be Spanish or neat's leather.
> HUDIBRAS.

Birchgrove Press

—

2015

LETTER I.

My Dear Girl,

I know I have long promised you an account of the reason of my penchant for the rod, which, in my estimation, is one of the most voluptuous and delicious institutions of private life, especially to a supposed highly respectable old maid like your esteemed friend. Treaties must be carried out, and promises kept, or how can I ever hope for the pleasure of making you taste my little green tickler again. Writing, and especially a sort of confession of my voluptuous weakness, is a most unpleasant task, as I feel as shamefaced in putting these things on paper as when my grandfather's housekeeper first bared my poor blushing little bottom to his ruthless attack. My only consolation at commencing is the hope that I shall warm to the subject as it progresses, in my endeavour to depict, for your gratification, some of the luscious episodes of my early days.

My grandfather, as you well know, was the celebrated Indian General, Sir Eyre Coote, almost as well known for his eight-penny fiasco with the Bluecoat boys as for his services to the Hon. E. I. Company. He was a confirmed martinet, and nothing delighted him so much as a good opportunity for the use of the cat, but I cannot tell you anything about that, as that was before my time. My first recollection of him is after the aforesaid City scandal, when he had to retire from public life in comparative disgrace. My parents both died when I was just upon twelve years of age, and the old General, who had no other relatives to care for, took entire charge of me, and, at his death, I was left his sole heiress, and mistress of nearly £3,000 per annum.

He resided in a quiet country house some twenty miles from London, where I spent the first few months of my orphaned life, with only his housekeeper, Mrs. Mansell, and the two servants, Jane and Jemima. The old General being away in Holland searching, so I afterwards heard, for original editions respecting the practices of Cornelius Hadrien, a curious work on the flagellation of religious penitents by a father confessor.

It was the middle of summer when he returned, and I soon found the liberty I had been enjoying considerably restricted. Orders not to pluck the flowers, or the fruit in the garden; and a regular lesson set me every day by the old autocrat himself. At first they were tolerably simple, but gradually increased in difficulty, and now, in after years, I can plainly understand his wolf and lamb tactics, by which I must eventually fall under his assumed just displeasure.

What gave me considerable pleasure at this time was his decided objection to mourning, or anything at all sombre in my dress. He said my parents had been shown every possible respect by wearing black for months, and I must now be dressed as became a young lady of my good expectations.

Although we scarcely ever received company, and then only some old fogy of his military acquaintance, I was provided with a profusion of new and elegant dresses, as well as beautiful shoes, slippers, drawers, and underlinen, all trimmed with finest lace &c., not even forgetting some very beautiful garters, a pair of which with gold buckles, he would insist upon putting on for me, taking no notice of my blushing confusion, as he pretended to arrange my drawers and skirts afterwards, but merely to remark:

What a fine figure I should make, if they ever had to strip me for punishment.

Soon my lessons began to be harder than I could fairly manage. One day he expostulated, "Oh! Rosa; Rosa!! why don't you try to be a better girl. I don't want to punish you."

"But grandfather," I replied, "how can I learn so much of that horrid French every day. I'm sure no one else could do it."

"Hold your tongue, Miss Pert, I must be a better judge than a little girl like you."

"But, grandfather dear, you know I do love you, and I do try my best."

"Well, prove your love and diligence in future, or your posterior must feel a nice little birch, I shall get ready for you," said he sternly.

Another week passed, during which I could not help observing an unusual fire and sparkle in his eyes, whenever I appeared in evening dress at the dinner table (we always dined in quiet state), and he also suggested that I ought to wear a choice little bouquet of fresh flowers in my bosom, to set off my complexion.

But the climax was approaching, I was not to escape long; he again found fault, and gave me what he gravely called one last chance: my eyes were filled with tears, and I trembled to look at his stern old face, and knew any remonstrance on my part would be useless.

The prospect of punishment made me so nervous, it was with the greatest difficulty I could attend to my lessons, and the second day after, I broke down entirely.

"Oh! Ho! it's come to this has it, Rosie?" said the old gentleman, "nothing will do, you must be punished."

Ringing the bell for Mrs. Mansell, he told her to have the punishment room and the servants all ready, when he should want them, as he was sorry to say "Miss Rosa was so idle, and getting worse and worse with her lessons every day, she must now be taken severely in hand or she would be spoiled for life."

"Now, you bad girl," said he, as the housekeeper retired, "go to your room and reflect upon what your idleness has brought to you."

Full of indignation, confusion, and shame, I rushed to my chamber, and bolted the door, determined they should break the door down first before I would submit to such a public exposure, before the two servants; throwing myself on the bed, I gave vent to my tears for at least a couple of hours, expecting every moment the dreadful summons to attend the old man's punishment drill, as he called it, but, no one disturbing me, I at last came to the conclusion it was only a plan of his to frighten me, and so I fell into a soothing sleep. A voice at the door awakened me, and I recognized the voice of Jane, as she said, "Miss Rosa, Miss Rosa, you'll be late for dinner."

"No dinner for me, Jane, if I'm going to be punished; go away, leave me alone," whispered I through the keyhole.

"Oh! Miss Rosie, the General's been in the garden all the afternoon, quite good-tempered, perhaps he's forgotten it all; don't make him angry by not being ready for dinner, let me in quick."

So I cautiously drew the bolt, and let her assist me to dress.

"Cheer up, Miss Rosie, don't look dull, go down as if nothing had happened, and most likely all will be forgotten; his memory is so short, especially if you put in your bosom this sweet little nosegay to please him, as you have never done it since he said it would set off your complexion."

Thus encouraged, I met my grandfather with a good appetite, and, as if the "bitterness was past," like Agag before Samuel, little suspecting I should be almost hewed in pieces afterwards.

The dinner passed most pleasantly, for such a formal affair as my grandfather made it, he took several glasses of wine, and in the middle of the dessert seemed to contemplate me with unusual interest; at last suddenly seeming to notice the little bouquet of damask and white roses, he said, "That's right, Rosa, I see you have carried out my suggestion of a nosegay at last; it quite improves your appearance, but nothing to what my birch will effect on your naughty bottom, which will soon look like

8

one of those fine peaches, and now's the time to do it," said he, ringing the bell.

Almost distracted, and ready to faint, I rushed for the door, but only in time to fall into the arms of strong Jemima.

"Now for punishment drill; march on, Jemima, with the culprit, you've got her safe; Mrs. Mansell and Jane, come on," said he to them, as they appeared in the background.

Resistance was useless. I was soon carried into a spare room I had never entered; it contained very little furniture, except the carpet, and one comfortable easy chair; but on the walls hung several bunches of twigs, and in one corner stood a thing like a stepladder, but covered with red baize, and fitted with six rings, two halfway up, two at bottom, and two at the top.

"Tie her to the horse, and get ready for business," said the General, as he seated himself in the chair, to look on at his ease.

"Come, Rosa, dear, don't be troublesome, and make your grandfather more angry," said Mrs. Mansell, unfastening my waistband. "Slip off your dress, whilst the girls put the horse in the middle of the room."

"Oh! No! No! I won't be whipped," I screamed. "Oh! Sir! Oh! Grandfather, do have mercy," said I, throwing myself on my knees before the old man.

"Come, come, it's no use showing the white feather, Rosa, it's for your own good. No more nonsense. Mrs. Mansell, do your duty, and let us get the painful business over; she isn't one of my stock if she doesn't show her pluck when it comes to the pinch."

The three women all tried to lift me, but I kicked, scratched, and bit all round, and, for a moment or two, almost beat them off in my fury, but my strength was soon exhausted, and Jemima, smarting from a severe bite, carried me in vengeful triumph to the dreaded machine. Quick as thought, my hands and feet were secured to the upper and lower rings; the horse widening towards the ground caused my legs to be well apart when drawn up closely to the rings at my ankles.

I could hear Sir Eyre chuckle with delight, as he exclaimed,

"By God! she's a vixen, and it must be taken out of her, she's a Coote all over. Bravo, Rosie! Now get her ready quickly."

I submitted in sullen despair, whilst my torn dress and underskirts were turned up and pinned round my shoulders, but when they began to unloose my drawers, my rage burst out afresh, and turning my head, I saw the old man, his stern face beaming with pleased animation, whisking in his right hand a small bunch of fresh birchen twigs. My blood was in a boil, and my bottom tingled with anticipated strokes, especially when Jemima, pulling the drawers nearly down to my knees, gave me a smart little slap on the sly, to let me know what I might soon expect, and I fairly shouted, "You must be a cruel old beast to let them treat me so."

"Old beast, indeed!" said he, jumping up in a passion. "We'll see about that, Miss; perhaps you'll be glad to apologize before long."

I saw him stepping forward. "Oh! Mercy! Mercy! Sir! I didn't mean it; they've hurt me so; I couldn't help what I said."

"This is a really serious case," said he, apparently addressing the others. "She's idle, violently vicious, and even insulting to me, her only natural guardian, instead of treating me with proper respect. There can be no alternative, the only remedy, however painful the scene may be to us who have to inflict the punishment, is to carry it out, as a matter of duty, or the girl will be ruined. She has never been under proper control all her life."

"Oh! Grandfather, punish me any way but this. I know I can't bear it; it's so dreadfully cruel," I sobbed out through my tears.

"My child, such crocodile tears have no effect on me; you must be made to feel the smart. If we let you off now, you would be laughing at it all, and go on worse than before. Stand aside, Jane, we can't waste any more time." So saying, he made a flourish with the rod, so as to make quite an audible "whisk" in the air. I suppose it was only to clear the way, as it did not touch me; in fact up to this time, he had treated me like a cat which knows the poor mousey cannot escape, but may be pounced upon at any time.

I could see the tears in Jane's eyes, but Jemima had a malicious smile on her face, and Mrs. Mansell looked very grave, but no time was allowed for reflections; the next instant I felt a smart but not heavy stroke right across my loins, then another, and another, in rather quick succession, but not too fast for me to think that perhaps after all it would not be so dreadful as I feared; so setting my teeth firmly without uttering a word, I determined to give as little indication as possible of my feelings. All this and a great deal more flashed through my brain before six strokes had been administered, my bottom tingled all over, and the blood seemed to rush like lightning through my veins at every blow, and my face felt as my poor posteriors.

"Now, you idle puss," said the General, "you begin to feel the fruits of your conduct. Will you? Will you call me an old beast again?" giving a harder stroke at each ejaculation.

My courage still sustained my resolution not to cry out, but only seemed to make him more angry.

"Sulky tempered and obstinate, by Jove!" he continued; "we must draw it out of you. Don't think, Miss, I'm to be beaten by a little wench like you; take that, and that, and that," whisking me with still greater energy, concluding with a tremendous whack which drew up the skin to bursting tension, and I felt another like it would make the blood spurt forth, but he suddenly paused in his fury, as if for want of breath, but as I now know too well, only to prolong his own exquisite pleasure.

Thinking all was over, I entreated them to let me go, but to my sorrow soon found my mistake.

"Not yet, not yet, you bad girl, you're not half punished for all your biting, scratching, and impudence," exclaimed Sir Eyre.

Again the hateful birch hissed through the air, and cut into my bruised flesh, both buttocks and thighs, suffering and smarting in agony, but he seemed careful at first not to draw the blood; however, I was not to escape, it was only his deliberate plan of attack, so as not to exhaust the poor victim too soon.

"Bite, and scratch, and fight against my orders again, will you? Miss Rosie, you'll know next time what to expect. You deserve no mercy, the idleness was bad enough, but such murderous conduct is awful; I believe you would have killed anyone in your passion if you could. Bite, scratch, and fight, eh! Bite, will you?" Thus lectured the old man, getting warmer and warmer in his attack, till the blood fairly trickled down my poor thighs.

I was in dreadful agony at every cut, and must have fainted, but his lecturing seemed to sustain me like a cordial; besides, with the pain I experienced a most pleasurable warmth and excitability impossible to be described, but which, doubtless, you, my dear, have felt for yourself when under my discipline.

But all my fortitude could not much longer suppress my sighs and moans, and at last I felt as if I must die under the torture, in spite of the exquisite sensation which mingled with it; notwithstanding my ohs and ahs, and stifled cries, I would not ask for mercy again; my sole thoughts ran upon the desire for vengeance, and how I should like to whip and cut them all in pieces, especially the General and Jemima, and even poor tearful Jane.

Sir Eyre seemed to forget his age, and worked away in frightful excitement.

"Damme, won't you cry for mercy? Won't you apologize, you young hussey," he hissed between his teeth. "She's tougher and more obstinate than any of the family, a real chip of the old block. But to be beaten by the young spitfire, Mrs. Mansell, is more than I can bear. There! there! there!" cried he; and at last the worn-out stump of the rod fell from his hand, as he sank back quite exhausted in his chair.

"Mrs. Mansell," he gasped, "give her half-a-dozen good stripes with a new rod to finish her off, and let her know that although she may exhaust an old man, there are other strong arms that can dispense justice to her impudent rump."

The housekeeper, in obedience to the command, takes up a fine fresh birch, and cuts deliberately, counting, in clear voice, one, two, three, four, five, six (her blows were heavy, but did not seem to sting so cruelly as those given by Sir Eyre). "There," she says, "Miss Rosa, I might have laid it on more heavily, but I pitied you this first time."

Nearly dead, and frightfully cut up, although victorious, I had to be carried to my room. But what a victory? all torn and bleeding, as I was, besides the certainty that the old General would renew his attack the first favourable opportunity.

Poor Jane laughed and cried over my lacerated posteriors as she tenderly washed me with cold arnica and water, and she seemed so used to the business that when we retired to rest (for I got her to sleep with me) I asked her if she had not often attended bruised bottoms before.

"Yes, Miss Rosie," she replied; "but you must keep the secret and not pretend to know anything. I have been whipped myself, but not so bad as you were, although it's cruel. We all rather like it after the first time or two; especially if we are not cut up too much. Next time you should shout out well for mercy, &c., as it pleases the old man, and he won't be so furious. He was so bad and exhausted with whipping you, Mrs. Mansell was going to send for the doctor, but Jemima said a good birching would do him more good, and draw the blood away from his head; so they pickled him finely, till he quite came to himself, and begged hard to be let off."

Thus ended my first lesson; and, in further letters, you shall hear how I got on with Jane, continued the contest with the General, my adventures at Mrs. Flaybum's school, and my own domestic discipline since left to myself.

Believe me, Dear Nellie,
Your affectionate friend
ROSA BELINDA COOTE.

LETTER II.

My Dear Nellie,

To continue my tale where I left off. Jane and I had some further conversation next morning, which, to the best of my recollection, was as follows:—

ROSA.—"So, Jane, you have been whipped, have you. What was it for?"

JANE.—"The first time was for being seen walking with a young man coming from church. The General said I had never been, and only pretended to be religious for the chance of gadding about with young fellows, which must be checked, or I should be ruined."

ROSA.—"Well; didn't you feel revengeful at being whipped for that?"

JANE.—"So I did, but forgot all about it in the delight I had in seeing Jemima well cut up. Oh, she did just catch it, I can tell you; but she's as strong and hard as leather."

ROSA.—"So I could forget and forgive too, if I could but cut you all up well. I've got a good mind to begin with you, Jane, when I don't feel quite so sore."

JANE.—"Ah! But I know you hate Jemima, and would rather see her triced up to the horse. Perhaps we shall be able to get her into a scrape between us, if we put our heads together."

ROSA.—"Oh! you sly girl. Don't you think I'll let you off, much as I long to repay the others. Just wait till I feel well enough, and I'll settle you first. There will be plenty of opportunities, as you are to sleep with me in my room every night. I haven't forgotten how you persuaded me to dress for dinner, when you knew, all the time, what was coming."

JANE.—"Dear Miss Rosie, I couldn't help it. Mrs. Mansell sent me up to dress you. The old General put it off till after dinner, as he likes to see the culprits dressed as nicely as possible. If he punished any of us, we have to attend punishment drill in our very best clothes, and if they get damaged, Mrs. Mansell soon fits us out again, so we don't lose much by a good birching. I have known Jemima to get into trouble so as to damage her things, but Sir Eyre made her smart well for them."

I was very sore for several days, but managed to make and secrete a fine bunch of twigs, ready for Miss Jane when she would little expect it; in fact, she did not know I had been into the garden or out of the house. Of course she was a much stronger and bigger girl than myself, so I should have to secure her by some stratagem. I let her think I had quite forgotten my threat, but one evening, just as we were both undressed for bed, I said, "Jane, did Mrs. Mansell or Jemima ever birch you without grandfather knowing it?"

JANE.—"Yes, dear Miss Rosie, they've served me out shamefully, more than once."

ROSA.—"How did they manage that?"

JANE.—"Why, I was tied by my hands to the foot of the bedstead."

ROSA.—"Oh! Do show me, and let me tie you up to see how it all looked."

JANE.—"Very well; if it's any pleasure to you, Miss."

ROSA.—"What shall I tie you up with? You're as strong as Samson."

15

JANE.—"A couple of handkerchiefs will do, and there's a small comforter to tie my legs."

By her directions I soon had her hands tied to the two knobs at the foot of the bed, and her feet stretched out a little behind were secured to the legs of the table.

"Oh! My!" said Jane. "You have fixed me tight. What did you tie so hard for? I can't get away till you release me."

"Stay! Stay!" I cried. "I must see you quite prepared now you are properly fixed up"; and I quickly turned up her nightdress and secured it well above her waist, so as to expose her plump bottom and delicately mossed front to my astonished gaze.

"Oh! What a beauty you are, Jane," said I, kissing her, "and you know I love you, but your naughty little bum-bedee must be punished. It is a painful duty, but I'll let you see it's no joke, Miss. Look, what a fine swishtail I've got," producing my rod.

"Mercy! Mercy!" cried Jane. "Dear Miss Rosie, you won't beat me; I've always been so kind to you!"

"It won't do, Jane, I must do my duty. You were one of the lot against me, and the first I can catch. It may be years before I can pay off the others."

The sight of her beautiful posteriors filled me with a gloating desire to exercise my skill upon them, and see a little of what I had to feel myself. Nervously grasping my birch, without further delay, I commenced the assault by some sharp strokes, each blow deepening the rosy tints to a deeper red.

"Ah! Ah! What a shame. You're as bad as the old General, you little witch, to take me so by surprise."

"You don't seem at all sorry, Miss," I cried; "but I'll try and bring down your impudence; in fact, I begin to think you are one of the worst of them, and only acted the hypocrite, with your pretended compassion, when you were, in reality, it all the time. But it's my turn now. Of course, you were too strong for me, unless I had trapped you so nicely. How do you like it, Miss Jane?" All this time I kept on, whisk, whisk, whisk, in quick succession, till her bottom began to look quite interesting.

16

"You little wretch! You vixen!" gasped Jane. "Your grandfather shall hear of this."

"That's your game, is it, Miss Tell-tale. At any rate, you'll be well paid first," I replied. The sight of her buttocks only seemed to add to my energy, and it was quite a thrill of pleasure when I first saw the blood come. She writhed and wriggled with suppressed sighs and ahs, but each time she gave utterance to any expression, it seemed only for the purpose of irritating me more and more. My excitement became intense, the cruel havoc seemed to be an immense satisfaction to me, and her bottom really was in deplorable state through my inconsiderate fury. At last, quite worn out and fatigued, I could hold the rod no longer, and my passion melted into love and pity, as I saw her in an apparently listless and fainting condition, with drooping head, eyes closed, and hands clenched.

The worn-out birch was dropped, and kissing her tenderly, I sobbed out, "Jane, dear, Jane, I both love and forgive you now, and you will find me as tender to you as you were to me after my flogging."

Her hands and feet were soon released, when to my astonishment, she threw her arms round my neck as with sparkling eyes and a luscious kiss she said softly, "And forgive you too, Miss Rosie, for you don't know what pleasure you have given me, the last few moments have been bliss indeed."

This was all a puzzle to me at the time, but I understood it well enough afterwards. She made quite light of her bruised bottom, saying, "What was awful to you was nothing to me, Miss Rosie, I am so much older and tougher; besides, the first time is always the worst; it was too bad of Sir Eyre to cut you up as he did, but your obstinacy made him forget himself; you'll grow to like it as I do."

This and much more in the same strain passed as we bathed and soothed the irritated parts, and we finally fell asleep with a promise from me to let her give me a pleasant lesson in a day or two.

Things went on smoothly for a few days, my punishment had

been too severe for me to lightly dare a second engagement with the General; still I burned for a chance to avenge myself on anyone but Jane, who was now my bosom friend. We discussed all sorts of schemes for getting anyone but ourselves into trouble, but to no purpose. The old gentleman often cautioned me to take care, as the next time he should not fail to make me cry, "Peccavi."

One fine afternoon, however, being in the garden with the housekeeper, I remarked to her, "What a pity it was grandfather let the nectarines hang and spoil, and no one allowed to taste them."

"My dear," said Mrs. Mansell, "if you take two or three he'll never miss them, only you must not tell that I said so, it's a shame to let them rot."

"But, Mrs. Mansell, that would be stealing," I replied.

"When nothing's lost nothing can have been stolen; it's only a false sense of honesty, and you, the little mistress of the house," she urged.

"Well, you are the serpent, and I'm Eve, I suppose; they really do look delicious, and you won't tell, will you?" I asked in my simplicity; so the fruit was plucked, and Mrs. Mansell helped to eat it, which put me quite at my ease.

Just before dinner next day we were surprised by the General calling us all into his sitting-room, "How's this, Mrs. Mansell?" he said, looking fearfully angry. "I can't leave my keys in the lock of that cabinet without someone tasting my rum; I've long known there was a sly sipping thief about, so I have been sly too. Finding it was the rum that was most approved, the last time the decanter was filled I put a little scratch with my diamond ring, to mark the height of the liquor in the bottle, and have only used the brandy for myself. Look! whoever it is has got through nearly a pint in three or four days. Come here, Rosa, now Mrs. Mansell, and now Jemima," said he, sternly, smelling the breath of each in turn.

"Woman," he said, as she faltered and hesitated to undergo this ordeal, "I don't think you were a sneaking thief, if you really wanted a little spirit, Mrs. Mansell would have let you have it,

I dare say, as you have been with us some years, and we don't like change, but you shall be cured of thieving to-morrow; you should have been well thrashed at once, but we have a friend to dinner this evening, it will do you good to wait and think of what's coming. Be off, now, and mind the dinner's served up properly or you'll catch it in Indian style to-morrow, and be a curried chicken if ever you were."

Our visitor was an old fox-hunting colonel, our nearest neighbour, and my spirits were so elated at the prospect of Jemima's punishment that it seemed to me the pleasantest evening I had ever spent in that house.

All next day grandfather spent looking over the garden, and a presentiment came over me that the nectarines would be missed; if he had been so cunning in one thing, he might be in another.

My fears were only too well founded, for catching sight of me with the housekeeper, cutting a nosegay for the criminal's wear, he said, "Mrs. Mansell, you had better make another bouquet whilst you are about it, someone has been at the nectarines; do you know anything about it, Rosa?"

"Oh! Grandfather, you know I was strictly forbidden to touch the fruit," said I, as innocently as possible.

"Mrs. Mansell, do you know anything of it, as she won't give a direct answer," said he, eyeing me sternly.

I was covered with confusion, and to make it worse, Mrs. Mansell with affected reluctance to tell an untruth, confessed the whole affair.

"'Pon my word, a nice honest lot you all are, as I dare say Jane is like the rest; Mrs. Mansell, I'm astonished at you, and I think your punishment will be enough, when you consider how seriously I look upon such things, but as to that girl Rosa, prevarication is worse than a lie, such cunning in one so young is frightful, but we'll settle Jemima first, and then think of what's to be done."

Left in this state of uncertainty, I fled to Jane for consolation, who assured me it was a good thing Jemima stood first, as the old man would get exhausted, and perhaps let me off lightly, if I screamed and begged for mercy.

19

Thus encouraged, I managed to eat a good dinner, and took an extra glass of wine on the sly (I was only supposed to take one). Thus fortified I marched to the *punishment drill* with great confidence, especially as I so wished to see Jemima well thrashed.

When first I set eyes upon her, as she curtseyed to the General, who was seated in the chair, rod in hand, her appearance struck me with admiration; rather above medium height, dark auburn hair, fresh colour, and sparkling blue eyes, low cut dark blue silk dress, almost revealing the splendours of her full rounded bosom, the large nosegay fixed rather on one side under her dimpled chin, pink satin high-heeled shoes, with silver buckles; she had short sleeves, but fawn-coloured gloves of kid, and a delicate net, covering her arms to the elbows, took off all coarseness of her red skin or hands.

"Prepare her at once," said the General, "she knows too well all I would say. Here, Rosie, hand me down that big bunch of birch, this little one is no use for her fat rump. Ha! ha! this is better," said he, whisking it about.

Jane and the housekeeper had already stripped off the blue silk, and were proceeding to remove the underskirts of white linen, trimmed with broad lace; the bouquet had fallen to the floor, and presently the submissive victim stood with only chemise and drawers. What a glimpse I had of her splendid white neck and bosom, what deliriously full and rounded legs, with pink silk stockings and handsome garters (for the General was very strict as to the costume of his penitents).

I assisted to tie her up, and unfastening her drawers, Jane drew them well down, whilst Mrs. Mansell pinned up her chemise, fully exposing the broad expanse of her glorious buttocks, the brilliant whiteness of her skin showing to perfection by the dazzling glare of the well-lighted room. I gave her two or three smart pats of approval just to let her know I hadn't forgotten the slap she gave me, then drew aside to make way for Sir Eyre.

My thoughts were so entirely absorbed by the fascinating spectacle that I lost all remembrance of my own impending turn. Whack! came the big birch, with a force to have made her jump out of her skin, if possible, but only a stifled, "Ah—r—r—re!" and a broad, red mark were the results; the blood mounted to her face, and she seemed to hold her breath for each blow as it came, but the rod was so heavy, and the old General so vigorous, that in less than a dozen strokes her fair bottom was smeared with blood and bits of birch were lying in all directions. "Ah! Ah!! Oh!!!" she screamed, "do have mercy, sir, I can't stand it. Oh! oh! indeed I can't."

"You sly thief, don't think I'll let you off before you're dead; if I don't cure you now I shall lose a good servant," exclaimed Sir Eyre, cutting away.

My blood boiled with excitement of a most pleasurable kind, young as I was, and cruel as I knew it to be, no pity for the victim entered my breast; it is a sensation only to be experienced by real lovers of the rod.

"You like rum, do you, Miss?" said the General. "Did you take it raw or mixed? I'll make your bottom raw."

The poor old man was obliged now to sit down for want of breath. Mrs. Mansell, understanding his wishes, at once took his place with a fresh birch, without giving the victim any respite.

"She must, indeed, be well punished, sir. I'm sure they're never denied anything so long as they behave themselves," said she, with a stern relentless face; in fact, after a stroke or two, her light-brown hair was all in disorder from the exertion, and her dashing hazel eyes, and well-turned figure, made me think her a goddess of vengeance. "Will you? Will you do so again? You ungrateful thief," she kept on saying, with a blow to each question.

Poor Jemima moaned, sobbed, and sometimes cried out for mercy, whilst the blood fairly trickled down her thighs, but the housekeeper seemed to hear nothing, and Sir Eyre was in an ecstasy of gloating delight. This could not last long, however strong the victim might be. Becoming exhausted with her accumulated sensations, she at last fairly fainted, and we had to dash cold water over her face to recover her; then covered with a cloak, she was led off to her room, and left to herself.

"Now, Rosa," said the General, holding out a light green bunch of fresh birch, "kiss the rod, and get ready for your turn."

Hardly knowing what I was about, I inclined my head and gave the required kiss. Mrs. Mansell and Jane had me prepared in no time, as I was quite passive; and as soon as I was fairly exposed and spread-eagled on the horse, the old General rose to his task.

"You have seen how severe I can be, by Jemima's punishment," said he; "but, perhaps, you did not think your answer to me yesterday was any offense, and I am almost inclined to forgive you, but remember in future, if you get off lightly this time, a plain lie is better than prevarication. I think the last flogging must have done you great good, your conduct is quite different to-night. But now, remember—remember—remember!" he cried again, giving sharp, cutting strokes at each word. My poor bottom tingled with agony, and I cried loudly for mercy, promising to be strictly truthful in future; so, after about twenty strokes, he said: "You may go this time," finishing me off with a tremendous remembrance, which made me fairly shake with the concussion, and was the only blow which actually drew the blood, although I had some fine tender weals. This must finish my second letter. Believe me my true-born child of the rod,

Your loving friend,
ROSA BELINDA COOTE.

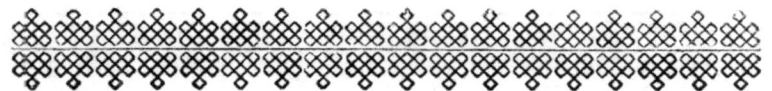

LETTER III.

My Dear Nellie,

I told you in my last how easily for me the affair of the nectarines passed over, but I was not long to go free with a whole skin. The General had evidently booked me in his mind for a good dressing the first time I should give him a pretext for punishment.

Strange to say, my first terrible punishment and dreadful cutting up of poor Jemima, related in my last letter, had very little effect, except, if possible, to render me rather more of a daredevil. I longed to pay off both Sir Eyre and Mrs. Mansell, but could think of no possible plan of effecting my revenge at all satisfactorily; if I could but do it properly, I was quite indifferent to what they might wreak upon me.

Jane could offer no suggestion, so I resolved to act entirely alone, and pretended to let it all drop, but sundry little annoyances were continually happening to different members of the family, even to myself. The General was very angry, and particularly furious, when, one day he found some of his flagellation books seriously torn and damaged, but could fix the blame on no one; indeed, I

23

rather fancy he strongly suspected Jemima had done it out of revenge. Next Mrs. Mansell got her feet well stung one night by nettles placed in her bed; she and Sir Eyre always were the principal sufferers, and, as a climax, two or three days afterwards, the General got his flesh considerably scratched and pricked by some pieces of bramble, cleverly hid in his bed, under the sheet, so as to be felt before they could be seen, it being his practice to throw back the upper bed clothes, and then, laying himself full length, pull them over him again. His backside first felt the pricks, which made him suddenly start from the spot, but only to get his hands, feet, legs, and all parts of his body well lacerated before he could get off the bed. I saw the sheet next day all spotted with the blood, for he was fearfully scratched, and pieces of the thorns stuck in his flesh.

Mrs. Mansell had to get out of bed in a hurry to attend the poor old fellow, and was occupied a long time in putting him to rights, retiring in about an hour's time, and making haste into bed, quite unsuspicious of any lurking danger (she had already been in it) when, prick—prick—prick! "Ah! my God! The devil's been here whilst I was away," she screamed. Jemima, Jane, and myself, ran to her room, and found her terribly scratched, especially on her knees; there were suppressed smiles on all our faces, and Jemima looked really pleased.

MRS. MANSELL.—"Ah! What a shame to serve me so. It's one of you three, and I believe it's Jemima."

JEMIMA.—"I couldn't help smiling, ma'am; you did scream so, and I thought you had no feeling."

MRS. MANSELL.—"You impudent hussey, Sir Eyre shall know of this." Jemima, Jane, and myself, all declared our innocence, but in vain; there evidently would soon be a grand punishment drill for her, if not for all three.

The housekeeper and the General were both too sore for nearly a week, and, in fact, many of the thorns remained in their flesh, and one in Mrs. Mansell's knee kept her very lame, Sir Eyre had to wait ten days before he could enter into any kind of an investigation.

At last the awful day arrived; we were all mustered in the punishment room, the General seated in his chair (it was after dinner, as usual), and we were all in evening costume.

SIR EYRE.—"You all know why I have called you together. Such an outrage as Mrs. Mansell and myself suffered from cannot be passed over; in fact, if neither Miss Rosa, Jemima, nor Jane will confess the crime, I have resolved to punish all three severely, so as to be sure the real culprit gets her deserts. Now, Rosa, was it you? for if not you, it was one of the others."

ANSWER.—"No grandfather, besides, you know all sorts of tricks have been played upon me."

SIR EYRE.—"Well, Jemima, what do you say, yes or no?"

JEMIMA.—"Good Lord, sir! I never touched such thorns in my life."

SIR EYRE.—"Jane, are you guilty or not, or do you know anything of it?"

JANE.—"Oh! Dear! No, sir! Indeed, I don't!"

SIR EYRE.—"One of you must be a confounded story-teller. Rosa, as a young lady, I shall punish you first. Perhaps we may get a confession from one of you before we've done."

Then turning to Mrs. Mansell, "Prepare the young lady; she didn't get such a birching as she ought to have had the other day, but if it takes all night, the three of them shall be well trounced. Jane and Jemima lend a hand."

My thoughts were not so much upon what I should feel myself, as the anticipation of the fine sight the others would present, and hoping to again realize the pleasant sensations I had experienced when Jemima was so severely punished. They soon removed my blue silk dress, and fixed me to the horse, but the General interposed; he had a different idea.

"Stop! Stop!" he cried. "Let Jemima horse her." So I was released, and having my petticoats well fastened over my back, I was at once mounted on her strong stout back, my arms round her neck, being firmly held by the wrists in front, and my legs also tied together under her waist, leaving me beautifully exposed and bent so as to tighten the skin. Mrs. Mansell was about to open my drawers when Sir Eyre says: "No! No! I'm going to use this driving whip. Jemima, just trot around the room. I can reach her now."

Then giving a sharp flick with the whip, which quite convinced me of its efficacy:—

"Now, miss! What have you to say for yourself? I believe you know all about it." Slash! Slash! Slashing with the whip, as Jemima, evidently enjoying it, capered round the room; each cut made my poor bottom smart with agony.

"Oh! Oh! Ah! Grandfather!" I cried. "It's a shame to punish me, when you know I'm innocent. Oh! Ah—r—r—re," as he slashed me without mercy. I could feel I was getting wealed all over, but my drawers prevented the flesh from being cut.

Presently he ordered a halt, saying: "Now, Mrs. Mansell, let's have a look at her naughty bottom, to see if the whip has done any good."

Mrs. Mansell, carefully opening my drawers behind, exclaims, "Look, look, sir, you've touched her up nicely, what beautiful weals, and how rosy her bottom looks."

SIR EYRE.—"Aye, aye, it's a beautiful sight, but not half pretty enough yet. Mrs. Mansell, do you finish her off with the birch."

I felt assured of catching it in good earnest now. The General lit a cigar, and composed himself in his easy chair to enjoy the scene. Mrs. Mansell selected a fine birch of long, thin, green twigs, and leaving my drawers open behind, ordered Jemima to stand in front of her.

Mrs. Mansell, whisking her birch, said, "I feel sure this young lady is in the secret, but we shall get nothing out of her, she is so obstinate, but I will try my best, Sir Eyre. Now, Miss Rosa, tell the truth if you want to save your bottom; are you quite as sure as ever of your own innocence?" whisking and slashing me smartly and with great deliberation, making the blows fall with a whacking sound, not inconsiderably adding to the previous warmth of my posteriors, which smart and tingle terrifically at each cut.

"Oh! ah! how unjust," I screamed, to relieve myself as much

as possible. "Oh, ah! If I do know I can't tell, it's a secret. Oh! have mercy!" thus trying to serve a double purpose to be let off lightly myself, by making them think someone else did it, and so transfer their fury to Jane and Jemima, whose whipping I hoped to enjoy.

MRS. MANSELL.—"Ha! ha! 'tis wonderful how the birch has improved you, my dear Miss Rosa, you're not nearly so obstinate as you were, but if you won't tell, you must be punished as an accessory. I'm sorry to do it, but it doesn't hurt you quite so awfully, does it?" thrashing away without a moment's respite; my poor bottom is beginning to be finely pickled, and I can feel the blood trickling down my legs inside my drawers.

"Hold! Hold!" cries the General, excitedly; "it's that devil Jemima; you've punished Rosa enough, try Jane next, if she knows anything we'll make her confess, and then the impudent red-headed Jemima shall catch it finely. We're getting at the truth, Mrs. Mansell."

I am let down, and the General orders Jane to take my place on the stout back; I let my clothes down with a thrill of excitement, and thanking Sir Eyre for his kindness, make myself busy in helping to arrange poor Jane's posteriors for slaughter, and pin up her skirts to her shoulders, exposing her fine, plump bottom, and beautiful thighs and legs, the latter encased in pink silk stockings, set off by red satin slippers and blue garters with silver buckles.

SIR EYRE.—"How now, Jane, you hussey, do you dare to come into my presence without drawers, how indecent, it's like telling me to 'ax my arse,' you impudent girl; how do you like that," giving her a tremendous under cut so that the birch fairly well wealed the flesh right up to her mossy crack; "it's all very well, in the heat of a birching, but to expose your nakedness like that so impudently is quite another," continuing to cut away in apparently great indignation.

JANE.—"Ah! Ah! Ah—a—r—re! My God, sir, have pity, Mrs. Mansell didn't allow us time to dress, and in the hurry I couldn't find my drawers to put on, and she was angrily calling me to come, and not keep her waiting. So I thought duty must be considered before decency. Oh! Oh! Oh! sir, you are cruel. Oh! have mercy, I'm as innocent as a babe!" as she is in terrible agony from the under cuts, which have already drawn the blood; she writhes and struggles so, Jemima can hardly stand under her plunging figure.

SIR EYRE.—"Well, well, I'm inclined to forgive you about the drawers, as I always like everybody to consider duty before everything, but how about putting the thorns in the bed; you must know about that, and it's your duty to confess."

JANE.—"Oh! Oh! Ah—r—r—re, I can't tell, I'm innocent, how can I split upon another? Oh, you'll kill me, sir! I shall be confined to my bed for weeks if you cut me up so!"

SIR EYRE.—"Fiddlesticks, bottoms get well quicker than that, Jane, don't be alarmed, but I shall punish you a good deal more if you don't confess it was Jemima did it. Now wasn't it Jemima? Wasn't it Jemima! wasn't it Jemima!" thundering at her both with voice and rod and drawing the blood finely.

The victim is almost ready to faint, still I could see the usual indications of voluptuous excitement, notwithstanding the agony she must be in, but at last she seems quite exhausted, and ceasing to writhe and wriggle as if she no longer felt the cruel blows whilst her shrieks sink to a sobbing. "Yes, yes! oh! yes."

SIR EYRE.—"Ha! Ha! Ha!" laughing in anticipation of getting the real culprit. "Yes! yes! she's confessed at last, let her down now, poor thing," throwing away the stump of the worn-out rod; "she took a lot before she would give way, but it's bound to come out."

Poor Jane is let down in a pitiable condition, and Jemima hisses something about "lying chit" between her teeth, as I assist Mrs. Mansell to tie her to the horse, and having pinned up her skirts, I opened her drawers so as fully to expose the snow-white beauties of her fine rump.

SIR EYRE.—"Open them as wide as possible, Rosa; the mean creature, to let others suffer for her own crime, and even take delight in helping to punish them."

JEMIMA.—"It's all a lie, Sir Eyre, I never had anything to do with it, and they have turned round on me so they may enjoy the sight of my flogging. Oh! oh! this is a cruel house, pay me my wages and let me go."

SIR EYRE, chuckling.—"You'll get your wages, or at least your deserts, you sneaking wretch."

JEMIMA (is crimson with shame and fury), exclaiming— "I'm not so much a sneak as somebody else who's done it; I'll die before I own what I never did."

SIR EYRE.—"Don't let us waste any more time on the obstinate hussey. Let's try what a good birch will do," slashing her two or three times severely on her bottom, and bringing out the rosy flush all over the surface of its firm broad cheeks.

"See how her bottom blushes for her," laughed the General, "but it will soon have to weep blood," increasing the force of his blows, and drawing weals at every stroke.

JEMIMA.—"Oh! Oh! Sir Eyre! how can you believe a lying girl like Jane, won't I box her ears for her when I get over this, the spiteful thing, to say it's me!"

SIR EYRE.—"You're the spiteful one. Will you box her ears? Do you really mean that, you strong, impudent donkey! I shall soon have to try something better than a birch on you, it's not severe enough; you shall beg Jane's pardon before I've done with you; you may be strong and tough, but we'll master that somehow; how do you like it? I hope you don't feel it, Jemima; I don't think you do, or you would be more penitent," said he, in a fury. "I wish I had a good bramble here to tear your bottom with, perhaps you might feel that."

JEMIMA.—"Oh! No! Pray don't. I didn't do it, and wouldn't have done such a thing to my worst enemy. Oh! Oh! Sir! Have mercy, I'm being murdered. You'll bleed me to death," as she feels the blood trickling down her thighs.

SIR EYRE.—"You're too bad to be easily killed. Why don't you confess, you wicked creature?" Then turning to Mrs. Mansell: "Don't you think, ma'am, she's got too many things on? I am not given to cruelty, but this is a case requiring greater severity than usual."

MRS. MANSELL.—"Shall we reduce her to her chemise and drawers, so you can administer the extreme penalty?"

SIR EYRE.—"Yes! Yes! It will give a little time to recover my breath. She's taken all the strength out of me."

We now strip all her petticoats off, and undo her stays, fully displaying the large fine plump globes of her splendid bosom, with their pretty pink nipples; then she is fastened up again, and stands with her wrists fastened well above her head. She has her fawn-coloured kid gloves, and the net, as usual, up to her elbows, so as to set off her arms and hands to the best advantage. She has nothing but chemise and drawers to hide her fine figure; but before commencing again, the General orders the latter to be entirely removed and her chemise to be pinned up to the shoulders; then turning to me, he said:

"Rosa, my dear, it's all through that wicked young woman you have been punished. I don't wish to teach anyone to revenge themselves, but as Mrs. Mansell is hardly well enough, and I am in want of a little more rest, I think you could take this whip," handing me a fine ladies' switch, with a little piece of knotted cord at the end. "There, you know how to use it; don't spare any part of her bottom or thighs."

This was just what I had been longing for, but did not like to volunteer. With a glance of triumph towards poor Jane (who was gradually getting over her own punishment, and beginning to take interest in what was going forward), I took the whip, and placed myself in position to commence. What a beautiful sight my victim presented, her splendid plump back, loins, and buttocks fully exposed to view, whilst the red wealed flesh of her bottom, smeared with blood, contrasted so nicely with her snow-white belly in front, ornamented on the Mons Veneris with a profusion of soft curly hair of a light sandy colour; and her legs being fixed widely apart, I could see her pink bottom-hole, and the pouting lips of her cunny just underneath; further down stretched the splendid expanse of her well-developed thighs, as white as her belly; then she was also dressed in crimson silk stockings, pretty garters and fawn-coloured slippers to match her gloves. My blood seemed to boil at the sight of so much loveliness, which I longed to cut into ribbons of wealed flesh and blood.

SIR EYRE.—"Go on, Rosie, what makes you so slow to begin? You can't do too much to such an obstinate thing; try and make her beg Jane's pardon."

ROSA.—"She looks very nice, but I'm afraid the whip will cut her up so, grandfather. Now, Jemima, I'm going to begin, does that hurt you?" giving her a light cut on her tender thighs, where the tip of the whip left a very plain red mark.

JEMIMA.—"Oh! Oh! Miss Rosa, be merciful; I've never been unkind to you; how nicely I rode you on my back when you were punished."

ROSA.—"Yes! and enjoyed the fun all the time, you cruel thing; you knew what I was getting, but I could tell you were delighted to horse me," giving three or four smart cuts across her loins, and registering every blow with a fine angry-looking weal. "There! There! There! Ask my pardon, and Jane's pardon for your threats. Will you box her ears, will you!" cutting sharply at every question in some unexpected part; no two strokes follow each other in the same place.

VICTIM.—"Ah—r—r—re, have mercy. I was sorry for you, Miss Rosie. Oh! You're as hard as Sir Eyre. You'll cut me to pieces with that whip," she sobs out, her face crimson with the conflicting emotions of fear, rage, and obstinacy.

ROSA.—"Now, Jemima, your only chance is to beg our pardon, and confess your crime; you know you did it, you know you did it, you obstinate wench," cutting the flesh in every direction, and making the blood flow freely all down the thighs on to her stockings.

The victim writhes and shrieks with pain at every blow, but refuses to admit her fault, or beg pardon. The sight of her sufferings seemed to nerve my arm, and add to my excitement, the blood seemed delicious in my eyes, and I gradually worked myself up, so that I felt such gushing thrilling sensations as to quite overcome me. The whip was dropped in exhaustion, and

I sank back on a seat in a kind of lethargic stupor, yet quite conscious of all that was going on.

SIR EYRE.—"Why, Rosie, I thought you were stronger than that. Poor thing, your punishment was too much for you. I'll finish the culprit. If she won't confess, she must be executed, that's all," snatching up another whip, much heavier than the one I had used, and with three tips of cord on the end. "You won't confess, won't you, you obstinate wicked creature? My blood boils when I think how I punished the other two innocent girls," he exclaimed, cutting her fearfully on the calves of her legs, knocking the delicate silk of the stockings to pieces, and wealing and bruising her legs all over. The victim cannot plunge about, as her ankles are fastened, but she moans with agony, and shrieks and sobs hysterically in turns at this terrible attack. The General seems beside himself with rage, for he next turns to her beautiful white shoulders, and slashes them about, fearfully cutting through the skin and deluging poor Jemima with her own blood.

SIR EYRE.—"I shall murder her; I can't help it; she's made me quite mad." His cuts wind round her ribs, and even weal the beauties of her splendid bosom, and stains the snowy belly with their blood.

JEMIMA (in low broken sobs).—"Oh! Oh! Mercy! Let me die! Don't torture an innocent thing like me any longer." She seems going to faint, when Mrs. Mansell interposes, saying: "It is enough; more may do serious injury."

SIR EYRE (gasping for breath).—"Oh! Oh! I know you are right to take me away, or I shall really murder her."

The bleeding victim is a pitiable and terrible sight as we release her from the ladder; she is scarcely able to stand; her boots covered with blood, and little pools of the sanguineous fluid stand on the floor; and we had to administer a cordial before she was able to be supported to her room, where she was confined to her bed for several days.

I had now had all the revenge I was so anxious to inflict; but the great avenger of all, to my great grief, soon removed poor old grandfather from this world, and left me indeed an orphan. Being still very young, my guardians under Sir Eyre's will placed me at Miss Flaybum's Academy to finish my education, and the old home was broken up, and inmates scattered.

I shall send you some of my school experiences in my next, and remain, Dear Nellie,

Yours affectionately,
ROSA BELINDA COOTE.

LETTER IV.

My Dear Nellie,

I promised in my last to relate a few of my school experiences, so now I will try and redeem the promise.

Her house was situated at Edmonton, so famous for Johnny Gilpin's ride. It was a large spacious mansion, formerly belonging to some nobleman, and stood in its own grounds. What were called the private gardens, next the house, were all enclosed in high walls, to prevent the possibility of any elopements.

Beyond these, in a ring fence, there were several paddocks for grazing purposes, in which Miss Flaybum kept her cows and turned the carriage horses, when not in use (which was all the week), for we only took coach, carriage, or whatever the conveyance might be, on Sundays, when we were twice regularly driven to the village church, nearly one-and-a-half miles distant, for Miss Flaybum's ladies could not be permitted, upon even the finest days, to walk there. We always called the vehicles coaches, although they were a kind of nondescript vehicle, and having nearly three dozen young ladies in the establishment, we filled three of them, and formed quite a grand procession as we drove up to the church door, and there was generally quite a little crowd to see us alight or take our departure, and, as the eldest girls assured us, it was only to see if we showed our legs, or displayed rather more ankle than usual. We were very particular as to silk stockings, and the finest and most fashionable boots we could get to set off our limbs to greatest advantage, and, in wet weather, when we were obliged to hold up our dresses rather more, I often observed quite a titter of admiration amongst the spectators, who curiously, as it seemed to us, were mostly the eldest gentlemen of the place, who evidently were as anxious to keep their sons away from the sight of our blandishments as Miss Flaybum could possibly wish; at any rate, it seemed to be understood to be highly improper for any young gentleman ever to present himself at what we called our Sunday levee.

We were never allowed to walk in the country roads, but on half-holidays or any special occasions, in fine weather, our governess would escort us into paddocks, and a little wood of three or four acres, which was included within the ring fence, where we indulged in a variety of games free from observation.

The school was very select, none but the daughters of the aristocracy or officers of the army or navy being admitted to the establishment; even the professions were barred by Miss Flaybum, who was a middle-aged maiden lady, and a very strict martinet.

Before I went to this school, I always thought such places were conducted with the greatest possible propriety as to morals, etc., but soon found that it was only an outward show of decorum, whereas the private arrangements admitted of a variety of very questionable doings, not at all conducive to the future morality of the pupils, and if other fashionable schools are all conducted upon the same principles, it easily accounts for that aristocratic indifference to virtue so prevalent in my early days.

The very first night I was in the house (we slept, half-a-dozen of us, in a fine large room), I had not been settled in bed with my partner more than an hour before quite a dozen girls invaded the room, and pulled me out of bed, to be made free of the establishment, as they call it.

They laid me across one of the beds, stuffed a handkerchief in my mouth to prevent my cries, and every one of them slapped my naked bottom three times and some of them did it very spitefully, so that my poor rump tingled and smarted as if I had had a good birching.

Laura Sandon, my bedfellow, who was a very nice kind-hearted girl of sixteen, comforted and assured me all the girls had to go through the same ordeal as soon as they came to the school. I asked her if the birch was ever used in the establishment.

"Bless you, yes," she replied; "you are a dear love of a girl, and I shall be sorry to see you catch it," kissing me and rubbing my smarting bottom. "How hot it is, let's throw off the bedclothes and cool it," she added.

"Let's look at her poor bottom," said Miss Louise Van Tromp, a fine fair Dutch girl; "shall we have a game of slaps before Mdlle. Fosse (the French Governess) comes to bed?"

"Yes, come, Rosa dear, you'll like that, it will make you forget your own smarts; get up Cecile and Clara for a romp," addressing the Hon. Miss Cecile Deben and Lady Clara Wavering, who with the French Governess made up the six occupants of our room. "You know Mdlle. won't say anything if she does catch us."

We were soon out of bed, with our nightdresses thrown off, and all quite naked: Laura, a thin, fair girl with soft large blue eyes, always such a sure indication of an amorous disposition; Cecile, about fifteen, a nice plump little dear with chestnut hair and blue eyes. Lady Clara, who was just upon eighteen, was dark, rather above the middle height, well-proportioned, with languid, pensive hazel eyes, whilst Louise Van Tromp was a fat Dutch girl of seventeen, with grey eyes and splendidly developed figure.

It was a beautiful sight, for they were all pretty, and none of them showed any shamefacedness over it, evidently being quite used to the game; they all gathered round me, and patted and kissed my bottom, Cecile saying, "Rosie, I'm so glad you've no hair on your pussey yet, you will keep me in countenance; these other girls think so much of their hairiness, as if they were old women; what's the use of it, Laura, now you have got it," playing with the soft fair down of Miss Sandon's pussey.

LAURA.—"You silly thing, don't tickle so, you'll be proud enough when you get it."

LADY CLARA.—"Cecile, dear, you've only to rub your belly on mine a little more than you do, that's how Laura got hers."

LOUISE.—"Rosie, you shall rub your belly on mine; Clara is too fond of Cecile. I can make yours grow for you, my dear," kissing me and feeling my mount in a very loving way.

LAURA.—"Listen to Grey Eyes Greedy Guts, you'd think none of us ever played with the Van Tromp. Rosie, you belong to me."

We now commenced the game of slaps, which in reality was similar to a common children's sport called "touch." Ours was a very large room, the three beds, dressing tables, washstands, &c., all arranged round the sides, leaving a good clear space in the centre.

LADY CLARA.—"I'll be 'Slappee' to begin," taking her station in the middle of the room.

Each girl now placed herself with one hand touching a bedstead or some article of furniture, and as Clara turned her back to any of us we would slip slyly up behind and give a fine spanking slap on her bottom, making it assume a rosy flush all over; but if she could succeed in returning the slap to anyone before they regained their touch, the one that was caught had to take her place as "Slappee."

We all joined heartily in the game, keeping up a constant sound of slaps, advancing and retreating, or slipping up now and then to vary the amusement, in which case the unfortunate one got a general slapping from all the players before she could recover herself, making great fun and laughter. You would think such games would soon be checked by the governess, but the rule was never to interfere with any games amongst the pupils in their bedrooms. Just as our sport was at its height the door opened, and Mdlle. Fosse entered, exclaiming, "Ma foi, you rude girls, all out of bed slapping one another, and the lamp never put out, how indelicate, young ladies, to expose yourselves so; but Mdlle. Flaybum does not like to check you out of school, so it's no business of mine, but you want slapping, do you? How would you like to be cut with this, Mdlle. Coote?" showing me a very pretty little birch rod of long thin twigs, tied up with blue velvet and ribbons. "It would tickle very differently to hand slapping."

"Ah! Mademoiselle, I've felt much worse than that three times the size and weight. My poor old grandfather, the General, was a dreadful flogger," I replied.

MADEMOISELLE.—"I thought girls were only whipped at school. You must tell me all about it, Miss Rosa."

"With great pleasure. I don't suppose any of you have seen such punishment inflicted as I could tell you of," I replied.

The young French lady had been rapidly undressing herself as this conversation was going on. She was very dark, black hair over a rather low forehead, with a most pleasing expression of face, and fine sparkling eyes, hid under what struck me as uncommonly bushy eyebrows. She unlaces her corset, fully exposing a beautiful snowy bosom, ornamented with a pair of lovely round globes, with dark nipples, and her skin, although so white, had a remarkable contrast to our fairer flesh. There seemed to be a tinge of black somewhere, whereas our white complexion must have been from an original pink source, infinitely diluted.

MADEMOISELLE.—"Ah! You Van Tromp, où est ma robe de chambre? Have you hidden it?"

LOUISE.—"Oh! Pray strip and have a game with us. You shan't have the nightdress yet."

MADEMOISELLE.—"You shall catch it if you make me play; your bottom shall smart for it."

We all gathered round her, and although she playfully resisted, she was soon denuded of every rag of clothing. We pulled off her boots and stockings; but what a beautiful sight she was, apparently about twenty-six, with nicely rounded limbs, but such a glorious profusion of hair, that from her head, now let loose, hung down her back in a dense mass, and quite covered her bottom, so that she might have sat on the end of it, whereas her belly, it is almost impossible to describe it, except by calling it a veritable "Forêt Noire." The glossy black curling hair, extending all over her mount, up to her navel, and hanging several inches down between her thighs.

"There, Mdlle. Rosa," she exclaimed, sitting on the edge of her bed, "did you ever see anyone so hairy as I am? It's a sign of a loving nature, my dear," nipping my bottom and kissing me as she hugged my naked figure to hers. "How I love to caress the little featherless birdies like you. You shall sleep with me sometimes. The Van Tromp will be glad to change me for Laura."

"We cannot allow that," cried two or three of the others together. "Now you shall be 'Slappee' with your birch, Mdlle."

"Very well," said the lively French lady. "You'll get well touched up if I do catch any of you."

Then we commenced our game again, and she switched us finely, leaving long red marks on our bottoms when she succeeded in making a hit. Her own bottom must have smarted from our smacks, but she seemed quite excited and delighted with the amusement, till at last she said: "Oh! I must be birched myself, who will be the schoolmistress?"

LAURA.—"Oh! Let Rosa! She will lecture you as if you were a culprit, and give us an idea of good earnest punishment. Will you, Rosa? it will amuse us all. Just try if you can't make Mademoiselle ask your pardon for taking liberties with you, do, there's a dear girl."

"Yes! yes! that will be fine," cried the others, especially Lady Clara, who was already seated on her bed with Cecile as her partner.

LOUISE.—"Mdlle. wants Rosa for her bedfellow to-night, so let her tickle her up with the birch; don't spare her, Rosie, she's so hard to hurt; come Laura, let us enjoy the night together."

Thus urged I took up the rod and, flourishing it lightly in the air, said, laughing, "I know how to use it properly, especially on naughty bottoms, which have the impudence to challenge me; now, Mdlle., present your bottom on the edge of the bed, with your legs well apart, just touching the floor, but I must have two of them to hold you down; come, Laura and Louise, each of you hold one arm, and keep her body well down on the bed, there, that will do just so, hold her securely, don't let her get up till I've fairly done."

ROSA.—"Mdlle. Fosse, you are a very wicked young lady to behave so rudely to me as you have done; will you beg my pardon, and promise never to do so any more; do you feel that and that?" giving a couple of stinging little switches across her loins.

MADEMOISELLE.—"Oh! no! I won't apologize, I do love little featherless chits like you!"

ROSA.—"You call me a chit, do you? I'll teach you a little more respect for your schoolmistress; is that too hard, or perhaps you like that better," giving a couple of slashing cuts on her rounded buttocks, which leave long red marks, and make her wriggle with pain.

MADEMOISELLE.—"Ah! Ah! Ah—r—r—re, that's too hard. Oh! Oh! you do cut, you little devil," as I go on sharper and sharper at every stroke, making her writhe and wriggle under the tingling switches which mark her bottom in every direction.

ROSA.—"Little devil, indeed, you shall beg my pardon for that too, you insulting young lady, how dare you express yourself so to your governess, your bottom must be cut to pieces, if I can't subdue such a proud spirit. There—there—there!" cutting away, each stroke going in on the tender parts of her inner thighs. "Will you be rude again? will you insult me again, eh? I hope I don't hurt you too much, pray tell me if I do. Ha! Ha!! Ha!!! you don't seem quite to approve of it by the motions of your impudent bottom," cutting away all the while I was speaking, each stroke with deliberation on some unexpected place, till her bum was rosy all over, and marked with a profusion of deep red weals.

Mademoiselle makes desperate efforts to release herself, but Lady Clara and Cecile also help to keep her down, all apparently highly excited by the sight of her excoriated blushing bottom, adding their remarks, such as, "Bravo, Bravo, Rosie, you didn't think she would catch it so, how delightful to see her writhe and plunge in pain, to hear her scream, and help to keep her down," till at last the surprised victim begs and prays for pardon, crying to be let off, with tears in her eyes.

This is the end of the night's amusements, for all now resume their night chemises and retire, Mdlle. taking me to sleep with her. "Ah! *Ma cherie,*" she exclaimed, as the lamp was put out and I found myself in her arms, "how cruelly you have warmed my poor bottom, and have you really seen worse than that, Rosie?"

"Oh! far, far worse, Mdlle., I've seen the blood flow freely from cut up bottoms," I replied, at the same time repaying her caresses and running my hand through the thick curly hair of her mount, as she was feeling and tickling my pussey. "There, there," she whispered, "nip me, squeeze that little bit of flesh," as my hand wandered to the lips of her hairy retreat, "tickle me as I do you," putting me in great confusion by her touches, for I had never experienced anything like it before, except the melting, burning sensations of the same parts at the conclusion of my previous flagellations.

This dalliance continued between us for some months, and I soon became an apt pupil in her sensual amusements, being emboldened by her freedoms, and heated by a most curious desire to explore with my fingers everything about that hairy paradise. Meanwhile she tickled and rubbed the entrance of my slit in a most exciting manner, and suddenly she clasped me close to her naked body (our chemises were turned up so we might feel each other's naked flesh), and kissed my lips in such a rapturous, luscious manner as to send a thrill of ecstasy through my whole quivering frame, her fingers worked nervously in my crack, and I felt quite a sudden gush of something from me, wetting her fingers and all my secret parts, whilst she pressed me more and more, wriggling and sighing, "Oh! oh! Rosa, go on, rub, rub"; then suddenly she stiffened herself out straight and seemed almost rigid as I felt my hand deluged with a profusion of warm, thick, sticky stuff.

After a few moments' rest she recovered herself, and said to me: "Listen! listen! The others are all doing the same. Can't you hear their sighs? Oh! Isn't it nice, Rosa dear?"

"Yes! Yes!" I whispered, in a shamefaced manner, for I seemed to know we had indulged in some very improper proceeding. "Oh! Mademoiselle, do they all do it? It's so nice of you to play with me so."

MADEMOISELLE.—"Of course they do. It's the only pleasure we can have in school. Ah! You should be with Lady Clara or the Van Tromp, how they spend and go on in their ecstasy."

"What is spending?" I whispered. "Is that the wet I felt on my fingers when you stiffened yourself out?"

MADEMOISELLE.—"Yes, and you spent too, little bashful. Didn't the birching make you feel funny?"

ROSA (in a whisper).—"Even when I have been cut so that the blood flowed down my legs, at last I suddenly got dulled to the pain, and came all over with a delicious hot burning melting feeling which drowned every other sensation."

MADEMOISELLE.—"Rosa, you're a little darling. Would you like to feel it over again? I know another way, if you only do to me exactly as I do to you, will you?"

I willingly assented to the lovely Française, who, reversing our positions, laid on her back, and made me lay my body on hers, head downwards. Our chemises were turned up close under our arms, so as fully to enjoy the contact of our naked bodies, and I found my face buried in the beautiful mossy forest on her mount, and felt Mademoiselle, with her face between my thighs, tickling my little slit with something soft and warm, which I soon found out was her tongue. She passed it lovingly along the crack and inside as far as it would reach, whilst one of her fingers invaded my bottom-hole, and worked in and out in a most exciting way.

Not to be behind hand, I imitated all her movements, and burying my face between her thighs, revelled with my tongue and fingers in every secret place. She wriggled and tossed her bottom up and down, especially after I had succeeded in forcing a finger well up the little hole and worked it about, as she was doing to me. Although it was all so new to me, there was something so exciting and luscious in it all; to handle, feel, and revel in such a luxuriously covered pussey and bottom excited me more and more every moment; then the fiery touches of her tongue on my own burning orifices so worked me up that I spent all over her mouth, pressing my slit down upon her in the most lascivious manner, just as her own affair rewarded me in the same manner. After a little time we composed ourselves to sleep, and with many loving expressions and promises of future enjoyment.

This was my experience the first night of my school life, and I need not weary you with repetitions of the same kind of scene, but simply tell you that it was enacted almost every night, and that we constantly changed our partners, so that was the cause of my acquiring such a penchant for female bedfellows, especially when they have been previously well warmed by a little preparatory flagellation.

Miss Flaybum was a stern disciplinarian in her school, and we often came under her hands, when she wielded the birch with great effect, generally having the culprit horsed on the back of a strong maid servant, who evidently delighted in her occupation.

I must be drawing this letter to a close, but will give you one illustration of how we were punished in my time.

I cannot exactly remember what my offense was, but it was probably for being impertinent to Miss Herbert, the English governess, a strict maiden lady of thirty, who never overlooked the slightest mark of disrespect to herself.

Miss Flaybum would seat herself in state upon a kind of raised dais, where she usually sat when she was in the schoolroom. Miss Herbert would introduce the culprit to her thus:

MISS HERBERT.—"Madame, this is Miss Coote, she has been disrespectful to me, and said I was an old frump."

MISS FLAYBUM.—"That is a most improper word to be used by young ladies, you have only to take away the f, and what remains, but a word I would never pronounce with my lips, it's too vulgar. Miss Rosa Belinda Coote (she always addressed culprits by their full name), I shall chastise you with the rod; call Maria to prepare her for punishment."

The stout and strong Maria immediately appears and conducts me into a kind of small vestry sacred to the goddess of flagellation, if there is such a deity; there she strips off all my clothes, except chemise and drawers, and makes me put on a kind of penitential dress, consisting of a white mobcap and a long white garment, something like a nightdress; it fitted close up round the throat with a little plain frill round the neck and down the front, being fastened by a band round the waist.

Maria now ushers me again into the presence of Miss Flaybum, all blushing as I am at the degrading costume, and ridiculous figure I must look to my schoolfellows, who are all in a titter.

Maria lays a fine bunch of fresh birch twigs (especially tied up with ribbons) at my feet, I have to pick it up and kiss it in a most respectful manner, and ask my schoolmistress to chastise me properly with it. All this was frightfully humiliating, especially the first time, for however free we might have been with one another in our bedrooms there was such a sense of mortifying shame, sure to be felt all through the proceedings.

Miss Flaybum, rising with great dignity from her seat, motions with her hand, and Miss Herbert assisted by the German governess, Frau Bildaur, at once mounted me on Maria's broad back, and pinned up the dress above my waist, then the English governess with evident pleasure opened my drawers behind so as to expose my bare bottom, whilst the soft-hearted young German showed her sympathy by eyes brimming with tears.

MISS FLAYBUM.—"I shall administer a dozen sharp cuts, and then insist upon your begging Miss Herbert's pardon," commencing to count the strokes one by one, as she whisks steadily, but with great force, every blow falling with a loud "whack," and making my bottom smart and tingle with pain, and giving assurance of a plentiful crop of weals. My red blushing bottom must have been a most edifying sight to the pupils, and a regular caution to timid offenders, two or three more of whom might expect their turn in a day or two; although I screamed and cried out in apparent anguish it was nothing to what I had suffered at the hands of Sir Eyre or Mrs. Mansell; the worst part of the punishment was in the degrading ceremony and charity girl costume the victim had to assume.

The dozen duly inflicted, I had first to beg Miss Herbert's pardon, and then having again kissed the rod, and thanked Miss Flaybum for what she called her loving correction, I was allowed to retire and resume my own apparel. I could tell you about many punishment scenes, but in my next shall have the grand finale to my school life, and how we paid off Miss Flaybum and the English governess before leaving.

> And remain, dear Nellie,
> Your ever loving
> ROSA BELINDA COOTE.

LETTER V.

———

My Dear Nellie,

I was nearly four years with Miss Flaybum before my education was considered to be complete. The last half-year had arrived, and you may be sure how I looked forward to my emancipation from the thralldom of Miss Herbert and her mistress; Lady Clara, Laura, and the Van Tromp had all left. Cecile now was my bosom friend, we had both grown our feathers as they were called, and I loved Mademoiselle Fosse so dearly that my guardians had arranged with her to live with me as a companion in future, as they intended making me a sufficient allowance to set up a genteel household of my own. Besides myself and Cecile there were at school no less than nine or ten big young ladies, who as well as Mademoiselle would leave for good when we broke up for the approaching Christmas holidays. Miss Flaybum seemed to be much annoyed at the prospect of losing quite a third of her pupils all at once; she became decidedly spiteful in her little tyranny, and in the punishments inflicted, seeming to take an especial delight in horsing the biggest girls; we were birched for the most trifling offences, often in threes and fours at a time;

46

such doings could not fail to breed resentment in our breasts, and we all longed for some chance of revenge. I had become quite a leader in the school, and with the other girls often made what we called sacrifices to the rod, especially of the younger pupils, in our respective bedrooms, who dared not complain to Miss Flaybum for fear of worse happening to them.

The last few days were approaching, and in less than a week I hoped to take leave of old Edmonton for good, and not wishing to abandon the field without paying off old scores I had a consultation with Mdlle. and Cecile, as to the practicality of wreaking our revenge. The result was we engaged all the big girls who were leaving to help us, besides taking about a dozen more of the others into our confidence, who promised at least to remain neutral frightened spectators. Miss Flaybum in her careful wisdom had all the servants, except Maria, sleep in a distant part of the house, and a heavily barred door prevented all access for them to us at night.

Miss Flaybum also invariably gave the young ladies a breaking-up party the evening before they were to go home, so we determined to bribe Maria to forfeit her allegiance and aid in our treason; the plan being at the end of the evening's entertainment to seize upon Miss Flaybum, Miss Herbert, and Frau Bildaur, and well birch them all, especially the two former tyrants. We had no difficulty with Maria, who had recently drawn most of her wages. I promised her a handsome *douceur* and a place in my own establishment, which she gladly accepted, being as she said quite tired out with the Misses' tantrums.

She also agreed to provide everything necessary for our purpose, cords, and especially three of the penitential dresses to put on our victims.

The eventful evening arrived, the conspirators had agreed between themselves to irritate Miss Flaybum by making very free with her champagne, which upon such occasions was made a great display of, but very sparingly served out to the company. Maria, assisted by two other servants, was principal waitress, and at supper, by her connivance, nearly all of us took about three

47

glasses of the sparkling gooseberry, instead of one, as usual on such occasions. Miss Flaybum opened her eyes in astonishment as she saw us indulging in a second glass, but when she saw us still further encroaching on her profuse hospitality she fairly exploded, "Miss Coote, Miss Deben, I'm astonished at you; how dare you, Mademoiselle, to encourage those young ladies in such intemperance," rising from her seat in rage, "why half of my pupils will get intoxicated; Maria, remove those bottles this instant, you must have lost your head."

Maria, who had watched the storm brewing, had, just the previous instant, succeeded in dismissing the other two servants and well bolting the door leading to the domestics' quarters, having, with good tact, provided them with a considerable amount of refreshment, to regale themselves withal.

Perceiving the field was all clear, I rose up, glass in hand, saying, with a bow of mock deference, "Wait a moment, Maria, we are not quite ready to dispense with the champagne. Miss Flaybum, Miss Herbert, and you young ladies (looking round the table), we shall, many of us, part tomorrow morning, never to return to this happy establishment, and I, for one, feel sure you will all join with me in drinking a real bumper to the health of our much respected and beloved schoolmistress."

Miss Flaybum gasped with agitation, but subsided into her chair, as if resigned to her fate, and apparently unable to help herself.

The young ladies all received the proposal with rapturous applause; glasses were filled without stint.

"Now, then," I exclaimed, stepping on to my chair and placing one foot on the table, "we must drink to the health of such an illustrious and amiable lady, with all honours, in the Scotch fashion, one foot on the table, and throw your glasses over your shoulders as you drain them to the bottom, in her honour. To the health of Miss Audrey Clementine Flaybum,—

For she's a jolly good fellow,
For she's a jolly good fellow,
For she's a jolly good fellow,
 And so say all of us,
 And so say all of us,
 And so say all of us,
With a hip, hip, hurrah,
With a hip, hip, hurrah,
 Hurrah, hurrah, hurrah."
     (Crash of glasses)

My confederates joined and gave the health in regular chorus and, I must say, in rather a masculine manner.

"My God! my God!" screamed Miss Flaybum, as the glasses crashed on the floor, or wherever they fell, "the young ladies are all drunk; what shall I do, Miss Herbert, how awful, where did they learn all this pot-house slang?"

"What an insult!" I exclaimed. "Are we drunk, young ladies? Cecile, Mdlle. Fosse, will you stand still to be stigmatized as drunkards?" We all crowded round Miss Flaybum and the English and German governesses, the two former red with passion, whilst Frau Bildaur was trembling with fear.

"This is no laughing matter," I continued, "we have all been insulted. Miss Audrey Clementine Flaybum, our turn is come now, you shall be made to smart for this, and make a most abject apology for insulting a number of young ladies of the highest aristocracy, and you Miss Dido Herbert, shall be punished too because you evidently approved it all. I think we will begin upon Frau Bildaur, but I won't be hard upon her, as she is rather tenderhearted. Maria, do your duty, no retiring, strip them, and put the penitential garments on before us all here."

MISS FLAYBUM, now pale and trembling with rage and fear.—"How dare you address me so; Maria, clear the room of these impudent young ladies, they are all flushed with wine."

Her appeals to Maria are all in vain; she first strips and robes Frau Bildaur; the poor creature, ready to faint with fear and

49

shame, offers no resistance, but Miss Herbert is indignant, and resists strenuously, whilst Miss Flaybum is held down in her chair by half-a-dozen strong young ladies.

"Never mind about dressing that old frump," I exclaimed; "stretch her on the table, and turn up her clothes."

Almost by magic the supper table is half cleared, all the debris of the entertainment being swept to the other end of the table. The struggling victim is powerless as soon as Maria with the assistance of Cecile and Mdlle. Fosse resolutely drag her to the table; she is stretched over the mahogany, and Mdlle., having turned up her clothes and pinned them well up, sits on her shoulders, to keep her down, whilst one or two others hold her arms. Cecile opens her drawers and exposes a rather thin bottom, saying, "She's not very plump, dear Rosa, but no doubt you can make her squeak."

ROSA.—"Tear off her drawers and fully expose her, I must pay off all scores at once."

This is speedily done, the victim appeals for mercy and exclaims against such indecency, but in vain; whilst Miss Flaybum looks on in speechless horror, gasping and sighing with indignation, and the thoughts of what shameful indignities may be in store for herself.

ROSA, giving a light swish on the exposed rump.—"Have you got any feeling, Miss Dido Herbert? I hope this won't hurt you much, but you've been a spiteful old thing to us for a long time." Swish, swish, swish, harder and harder, till the devoted bum begins to get quite rosy. "Will you beg our pardon, and promise to be kinder to your pupils in future?" giving a whack with all her force, which weals and almost draws the blood.

MISS HERBERT.—"Oh! Oh! we never punished like that! Oh! shameful, Miss Coote!"

ROSA.—"How dare you, Miss Dido, tell me it's shameful, do you really mean what you say?" slashing away in earnest, and soon making little drops of blood begin to ooze from the bruised weals.

MISS HERBERT, sobbing hysterically.—"Oh! Oh! I didn't

mean to say that. Oh! Oh! Ah—r—r—re! Have mercy! My God! how cruelly you cut!"

ROSA.—"I thought you would come round, Miss Dido; pray, don't you admire my style of birching, don't you wish me to do it a little harder," keeping up a vigorous stroke all the time, and beginning to make quite a beautiful display of raw buttocks.

The victim shrieks with agony and cries for help.

ROSA.—"You may scream, it's delightful to hear it, and know you have some feeling. Will you beg our pardons now?"

MISS HERBERT.—"Oh! Yes! Yes! I will, I will. Oh! Oh! pray stop, pray have mercy, I'll never be unkind any more!" sobbing hysterically, "Oh, dear!" Oh, dear! I shall faint, I know I'm bleeding! Oh! dear Miss Coote, how can you be so cruel?"

ROSA.—"Do you think we're any of us intoxicated? Don't you think it was very improper and unladylike of Miss Flaybum to say what she did, and insult us so, just as we had done her a great honour; what do you think of it, Miss Dido?"

MISS HERBERT.—"Oh! Ah! Ah! Ah! Ah—r—r—re! Oh! it was so wrong of her! Oh! I do apologize. Oh! let me go. Oh, Mercy!" as she writhes and twists in the most agonizing manner.

ROSA.—"You must thank me, and promise to retire quietly to your room when you are allowed to go, and profit by the lesson you have received; it is not half so bad as it might have been, there, there," giving her a couple of slashing undercuts between her thighs. "Kneel down and kiss the rod, and thank me."

MISS HERBERT.—"Ah! Ah! dreadful. Oh! I shall die! Oh! have pity," sobbing and moaning.

She is now released, and has to kneel and kiss the rod, and make most humble thanks, apologies, and promises, to the infinite delight of the audience, who thoroughly enjoy her humiliation as she kneels bathed in tears of pain and shame, and greet her with a storm of hisses as she slinks from the room crestfallen and smarting with her degradation.

ROSA.—"Now, Miss Audrey Clementine Flaybum, it's your turn; resist us, and you shall be punished ten times worse than that woman Herbert."

The schoolmistress is quite cowed by the previous scene. She implores for mercy, and begs them not to degrade her before the whole school, but Rosa and her accomplices are determined and relentless.

Maria gradually strips her mistress, who is a fine looking woman of the fat, fair and forty class, with quite prominent blue eyes and flaxen hair. The disrobing process displays in turn her fine neck and bosom, crimson with shame and heaving with agitation, whilst tears of bitter vexation course down her cheeks. Then she presently stands with only chemise and drawers, the latter so well filled out as to give promise of a splendid bottom within, and the ends beautifully trimmed with expensive lace, below which are seen a fine pair of plump legs, in flesh-coloured silk stockings, and high-heeled shoes, with jewelled buckles, but when the penitential-dress and mobcap are assumed, she looks quite a benevolent Mrs. Fry, grieving over some kind of human depravity.

"There," said Rosa, "she's wise not to resist. Let her stand and see Frau Bildaur receive her punishment, and I will rest too; you dear Cecile, take a new rod and punish her lightly."

It was a beautiful sight to see the chestnut-haired, plump, merry-looking Cecile as she whisked her birch against the trembling Frau, who was presently horsed on Maria's back, and, with drawers let down and skirts up, was soon ready for her punishment, displaying a very fine, full bottom on which to operate.

CECILE.—"Frau Augusta Bildaur, I will only give you a dozen smart cuts, and let you go, when you kiss the rod, and thank me for chastising you."

Thus saying, she slowly counts the number of each blow, as she strikes her well-aimed, deliberate cuts, which quickly raise all the exposed surface to a warm, rosy tint, and leave a lot of very red marks.

The victim receives her punishment very firmly, with closed lips all the while, but when released is very profuse in her thanks, as she kisses the instrument of her flagellation. The timid look is gone, and instead of the tears, her eyes are lighted up with a warm sensual light, and she begs, in a whisper, to be allowed to witness Miss Flaybum's castigation.

ROSA.—"What a pity there is no proper whipping post to tie her up to: we must make shift with the table. Put Miss Flaybum up in the same way as you did Miss Herbert."

The victim does not resist, as she sees it is quite hopeless, and would only entail greater pain on herself. Her drawers are removed altogether, displaying to the curious girls a beautiful plump bottom and white belly, ornamented by a fine Mons Veneris, covered with a profusion of light curly hair, with the tip of a luscious looking clitoris just peeping out between the lips of her pussey. They spread-eagle her on the table, four girls holding her legs wide apart, whilst others secure her arms, and Mademoiselle again sits on the victim's back to make sure of her.

ROSA.—"What a fine sight; how delightful to have to subdue the spirit belonging to such a splendid figure. Miss Audrey Clementine Flaybum, you have been guilty of grossly insulting myself and other young ladies, and you must retract all your accusations of drunkenness, and I trust to thoroughly convince you of our sober earnestness. Do I whip you like a drunkard, or were you not rather intoxicated with passion when you said so?" whipping her slowly at first. "Did we use pot-house slang? I hope I don't hurt your poor delicate bottom, it begins to look rather flushed, but perhaps it's only blushing at our rudeness," warming to her work, and slashing away in good earnest.

Miss Flaybum's face shows the depth of her indignation, whilst her fat, plump bottom writhes at every stroke, so that it is as much as the young ladies can do to hold her legs; she seems determined not to cry out, but Rosa increases her pain with such skillful and maliciously planted strokes, she is compelled at last to sigh for relief.

ROSA, laughing.—"Ha! Ha! Ha! she's obstinate and won't answer; she wishes me to cut harder; Maria, get another good heavy birch ready, this one won't last long. I begin to think Miss Audrey Clementine Flaybum is really drunk herself (roars of laughter), or she would have the sense to apologize, but I'll bring her to her sober senses. How do you like that, and that, and that," cutting each stroke as to go in well between the cheeks of her bottom, and touch the pouting lips of her pussey, which could be quite plainly seen behind; they were indeed painful cuts, and elicited a sudden sharp cry of pain.

MISS FLAYBUM.—"Ah! Ah! Oh! Oh! How cruel. What fiendish creatures to cut me up so!"

ROSA, laughing again.—"Ha! Ha! she's just beginning to get sober, a little more will thrash all the champagne out of her; drunken people always accuse others of being drunk," cutting up her bottom, and making the blood run in little streams, so that it soon began to run down her thighs, and drip from the hairs of her pussey; the flagellatrix and her friends are getting quite excited at the spectacle, but not the least in sympathy with the victim, whose sufferings seem to afford them exquisite voluptuous sensations, many of the elder girls being stretched on the floor together, or in other positions of sensual enjoyment.

The victim now screams indeed for "Mercy, Mercy! Oh! Oh! Have pity, Miss Coote. Oh! Oh! I shall faint, I shall die."

ROSA, in a state of furious excitement.—"No, no, no fear of your dying, your fat bottom will stand a good deal more yet; you are too obstinate to be let off, the birch will keep you from fainting. Why—why—why—don't you apologize?" giving a terrific undercut between the tender surface of her thighs at every question, making the poor schoolmistress gasp and moan in agony; still her proud spirit refused to do what was required of her.

She is almost fainting, when Rosa, who is getting rather tired with her exertions, calls for a bottle of champagne. "Now, then girls," she exclaims, "she's so plucky we must drink her health again." In response to this call, half-a-dozen young ladies take a bottle each, and at a signal from Rosa, all the corks are fairly discharged at the bleeding bottom, which presents a famous mark, and elicits peals of laughter at the joke, as they drink to "the plucky old girl," who is humiliated more than ever at this unexpected indignity.

Rosa, refreshed, throws away the stump of the birch she has been using, and takes up another heavy swishtail.

"This is something like a rod. Will you, now, Miss Audrey Clementine Flaybum, beg our pardon, and own you were drunk yourself, or must I cut your fat rump in pieces? Aha! That's the vulgar word you would never allow your lips to mention. Perhaps you did not think you had such a thing as a rump yourself, when you used to birch and humiliate us." Whacking away with great earnestness all the while she is lecturing the victim, who screams and shouts in agony as the thundering strokes of the fresh heavy rod crash on her bottom, scratching and tearing the already bruised and bleeding skin in a frightful manner.

Miss Flaybum is almost done for, and really thinks she is going to die, and in an agony of fear and pain forgets the indignity of her position, as well as her firm resolves never to debase herself before her pupils. She screams for mercy.

"Mercy! Oh! Oh! Oh!" she sobs. "Let me go now, dear Miss Coote. Oh! I will beg your pardon. I must have been intoxicated myself. Oh! Forgive me, and I'll never say a word about this. Oh! Oh! Indeed I won't if you spare my life," sobbing in a low hysterical voice.

ROSA.—"And you will forgive us all, and thank us for making you sober again? Fie! Fie! Miss Flaybum. You were indeed overcome. Was it not so?" giving a sharp cut right up under her pussey, to keep her from fainting, and steady to her promises.

VICTIM.—"Yes! Yes! Oh! Ah—r—r—re! I'm sorry to have forgotten myself, and—and—I do thank you for correcting me with firmness. Oh! Oh! Have mercy now, let me kneel and kiss the rod."

What a pitiable object she looked, kneeling in front of me, as she kissed the broken stump of the birch, which was now well dyed in her own blood. Such a sight of abject terror and degraded, humiliated pride, as well as the burning shame of all she had to endure; her cheeks were stained with tears, and her face and neck blushing nearly as red as her still exposed bottom; for, to humiliate her as much as possible, she had to kneel with her clothes still pinned up behind.

I don't know what possessed me, but I felt such extraordinary excitement that I hardly knew what I was doing; my only idea being that she was getting off too easily. So, suddenly stooping, I said, "Ha! Ha! Miss Audrey Clementine Flaybum, you know what a good birching is like now. I must look and see how I have pickled your delicate rump for you. I haven't cut it up too much," passing my hand all over the raw lacerated posteriors. "It will be well in a week, although there is a good deal of blood. See, see," wiping my hand all over her face, to her intense shame and disgust, just as she was beginning to slightly recover herself.

This was the last indignity before we allowed her to retreat to her room.

As to ourselves, we were indeed intoxicated with success, so that I shall never forget the goings on of that last night at school, how the girls rushed about to each other's rooms, and revelled in every kind of lasciviousness one with another. Sleep was banished from our eyes, and nothing but the advent of breaking-up day put an end to our orgie of sensuality.

Miss Flaybum was not visible next day, and the only reference she ever made to our memorable scene of retributive justice was an enormous charge for damaged glass in my school bill.

This will end my letter for the present, but, dear Nellie, when I return from my tour, perhaps I can tell you a little more of my experiences.

Your affectionate friend,
ROSA BELINDA COOTE.

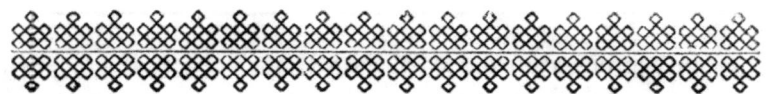

LETTER VI.

My Dear Nellie,

During my late tour in Italy and Germany I often amused myself with making notes for further letters to you on my return to England, collecting all the incidents I could think of or remember as likely to interest you, and now I am at home once more I will amuse myself on dull evenings by writing you another series of letters. Well, then, to begin.

When I left school my guardians entrusted me to the care of Mdlle. Fosse, and we were soon settled in a house of my own in the western suburbs of London. My establishment consisted of ourselves, Jane, my grandfather's late servant (who acted as our lady's-maid), a cook called Margaret, and two housemaids, Mary and Polly, besides a nice young page, a brother of Jane's who was called Charlie.

My guardians thought that until I was of age we could dispense with a footman or coachman, and hire from time to time such carriages as we might require to visit our friends, or go shopping, or to the theatres, and my allowance was limited to £1000 a year, out of which Mademoiselle had a liberal salary of £200, which

I never begrudged in the least; she was such a dear, loving soul, and always did all she could to further my amusements and keep me out of serious mischief.

Myself and Mademoiselle occupied separate bedrooms communicating with each other, so that we could, if we wished, enjoy each other's society by night as well as day. The cook and Mary occupied a room at the top of the house, whilst the page had a little cell of a room to himself on the same corridor as our bedrooms, and Jane and Polly (we were obliged to call her so, to distinguish her from the other Mary), were also in a room on the same flight, which also contained a couple of spare rooms for visitors. On the top floor there were several spare rooms, one of which was very large, and after consultation with Mademoiselle I determined to fit it up as a punishment chamber, and maintain strict discipline in my family. I had hooks fixed in the ceiling, and also provided a complete paraphernalia of ropes, blocks, and pulleys, a whipping post and ladder, also a kind of stocks in which to fix a body so as only to expose the legs and bottom behind, and prevent the victim from seeing who was punishing her.

Mademoiselle and myself frequently indulged in our *"Soirées Lubriques,"* as she called them, and for an occasional extra excitement, we got Jane, and either birched her in our bedrooms, or got her to assist us in birching one another, for I was now thoroughly given to the pleasures of the rod and the excitement to be raised by its application. These little bits of fun, as we called them, were wanting in that piquancy so appreciable when the victim is a thorough stranger to the birch, and feels its tickling effects for the first time. This made us particularly on the look-out for some culprit whom we might immolate to our prurient desires.

Our gardener was a steady man, rather over forty, and his wife, a very pretty woman of about thirty. They had two nice little girls of nine and ten years old, and lived in a small cottage at the back entrance of our garden, which was pretty large.

Mrs. White, the gardener's wife, was very fond of finery, and her husband's wages not being sufficient to satisfy her cravings in that respect, she hit upon the ingenious plan of supplying some of our neighbours (who were not so well off for garden produce as we were) with some of the fruit and vegetables which otherwise would have been wasted, and as she thought might as well be sold for her own profit. The father did not see much harm in it, as he afterwards said, Miss Coote was so good and generous, and did not seem to mind what they took for themselves.

The two little girls, Minnie and Lucy, were employed by their parents to carry things out at the back gate, but they happened to be seen by Jane early one morning, and duly reported to me.

I had long an unaccountable wish to birch these little dears, but could think of no excuse how to bring it about, so that Jane's report was most welcome.

In company with Mademoiselle, early in the morning, we repaired by a roundabout way to the back entrance of my garden, and placed ourselves so as to see exactly what was going on, and were soon rewarded for our trouble by seeing the little girls carry several baskets of fruits into their mother's cottage.

Having satisfied ourselves as to the facts of the case, I returned to the house, and ordered the gardener and all his family to be summoned to my presence.

In company with Mademoiselle, I received them in the drawing-room. White and his wife, leading in the little girls by the hand, and with a respectful obeisance, enquired the reason of my sending for them.

MISS COOTE,—"Your pretended innocence is well assumed. How is it, White, that your children carry away fruit from the garden as they do every morning?"

WHITE, stammering in great confusion.—"They only have a little for ourselves, Miss."

MISS COOTE.—"You're only adding falsehood to theft. White, your wife does not get all her finery out of your wages."

WHITE.—"Oh! Sally! (To his wife:) Pray speak. I don't know anything about it."

MRS. WHITE (scarlet with shame, and bursting into tears).— "Oh! Oh! It's all my fault. William don't know I ever sold anything, and the dear children are innocent. Oh! Pray forgive me, Miss Coote."

MISS COOTE (sternly).—"He must know. He's as bad as you, and you're bringing up those little girls to be thieves."

White and his wife and children all went on their knees, imploring me for mercy, and protesting that very little had been sold.

MISS COOTE.—"Nonsense! You make me think you even worse, because I know it has been going on for some time. Now make your choice. Shall I punish you severely myself, or have you taken before a magistrate? You know they will hang both of you."

White and his wife both implore for mercy, and beg me to punish them any way I may think best. "Only, only, pray Miss Coote, spare the dear little things, they only did what we told them."

MISS COOTE.—"You are wise to leave it to me. I may have some mercy; the law has none for poor wretched thieves. I don't know how to punish you, White, as you are a man, so I will forgive you, and hope you will be honest in the future; but Mrs. White and the children must be properly whipped and corrected. They must attend me here, dressed in their Sunday clothes, at seven o'clock this evening. Now you understand. Go home till then. I will cure them of thieving, or my name's not Rosa Coote."

Poor White and his wife are covered with confusion and retire for the present, whilst I congratulate Mdlle. Fosse on our good fortune in securing such victims.

Seven o'clock, and I am ready in the punishment chamber to receive the culprits. They enter with a very dejected appearance, although dressed smartly in the highest style of rustic fashion with their bouquets.

MISS COOTE.—"I am glad, for your sake, Mrs. White, you have left me to punish you, as I hope after this you will be thoroughly trustworthy. Mademoiselle Fosse, will you assist Jane in preparing Minnie for the birch? Stop! Tie Mrs. White to the ladder, or her motherly feelings may cause her to interfere, then get Lucy ready also. If they haven't got drawers on, we must find a pair for each of them."

MRS. WHITE (with tears in her eyes).—"Oh! Oh! Miss Coote, my dear young lady, don't be too hard on the children. Cut me to pieces rather."

She is soon tied by her wrists to the ladder, but left as she is, in all her clothes, for the present. Then they strip little Minnie and Lucy, and expose their pretty plump figures to our gaze. Mademoiselle takes Lucy on her knee, and I have the youngest, Minnie, only nine years old. The little creatures are all blushes, and quite crimson with shame as we turn them on our laps bottom upwards. They are evidently quite unused to inspection by strange ladies.

MISS COOTE (to Minnie).—"How you do blush, my dear; are you afraid I shall hurt you so much? What a lovely little bottom, does your mother often slap it?" giving two or three fair spanks, which very much improve the lovely colour of the firm flesh, and makes the little thing twist about beautifully, as she feels the smart.

MINNIE.—"Oh! Oh! Pray don't! How you hurt! I can't bear it, Miss Coote," beginning to cry, and the pearly tears dropping on my lap.

MADEMOISELLE.—"So you little girls sold the fruit for your mother; did you, Lucy?"

LUCY.—"Father gave it to us to carry home."

MADEMOISELLE.—"The old story of Adam and Eve. One tempted the other. So it was all father; mother quite innocent, eh?"

MISS COOTE.—"I think I can make Minnie tell us a different tale to that, Mdlle. Fosse. They are little story-tellers as well as thieves," giving Minnie a good slap with her open hand. "Just try my plan, Mademoiselle."

Minnie shrieks and kicks about in pain as Miss Coote slaps away, and Mademoiselle does the same by Lucy, till both their bottoms are as rosy as peaches. Both little girls screaming loudly for mercy; laying the blame first on father, and then mother, as they find it is no use to deny it.

"Now, Jane," says Miss Coote, "hand us a couple of light birches. We must thoroughly cure them before they are let off." Then taking hold of the birch, she directs Jane to tie both little victims to the whipping post, and puts a tight pair of drawers on each to hide their blushing rumps.

Jane ties them up, side by side, by their wrists, the arms well stretched above their heads, and their toes only just reaching the floor. Then she produces two little pairs of very thin lawn drawers almost as delicate as muslin, so that the rosy flesh was slightly perceptible through the material. They were, if anything, rather too small, and fitted quite tightly (the youthful bottoms are so finely developed, considering the age of their owners) and leave a space of nearly six inches wide behind, where they gave a delightfully seductive view of the pink roseate flesh and the cracks of the anus; altogether their shamefaced confusion and distress, as they gracefully lift their little legs, one by one, into the drawers, and go through all three positions Jane manages to put them in, as she fastidiously arranges them for sacrifice, was a most delightful sight to me, gloating as I was in the anticipation of the pleasure the whipping would be sure to afford.

MISS COOTE.—"Now, Mademoiselle, will you assist me in the whipping? I will do all the talking."

The mother here is so distressed at the sight of her children tied up for whipping that she tries to fall on her knees, but soon remembers herself, when her hands being tied up prevent her intention. "Oh! Oh! Miss Coote, do have mercy on my little girls," she sobs. "To think I should bring this on them. Oh! Oh!" trying to wring her hands.

MISS COOTE.—"Hold your foolish noise, woman. I'm just going to begin. How do you like it, Minnie? How is it, Lucy?" beginning to switch them finely, soon making a lot of thin red marks all over their backs and bottoms. "Will you ever take my fruit again, you little hussies? Warm their bottoms well for them, Mademoiselle. Take the thieving impudence out of their posteriors."

The victims shriek in a series of shrill screams, their faces are scarlet, and the tears roll in a little stream down their pretty pitiful faces, and they beg and pray to be let off. "Oh! Oh! we will be good, &c."

Miss Coote and her friend are delighted; the sight is so stimulating, their blood rushes through their veins and raises their voluptuous feelings of sensuality to the highest pitch, the cries of pain are so much music to their ears, and they cut the little bottoms dreadfully till the blood starts from the weals; the poor agonized mother is another spirit, which only adds to their enjoyment, as although only a spectator she seems to feel every blow, and cries and sobs as if her heart would break.

MADEMOISELLE.—"Look at the silly woman, you'll have something to cry for presently, Mrs. White."

The thin drawers are cut up, and torn into rags, the birches almost worn out, and the two flagellatrices would never have stopped, but Jane interposes, for little Minnie has fainted, and Lucy seems likely to go off too.

They untie them, and with a little water and pungent smelling salts soon revive the little one, then both mother and children are refreshed by some champagne, slightly dashed with a most stimulating liqueur.

Mrs. White, who had also been released, nurses her children on her lap, caressing and kissing them, crying and hysterically sobbing over their sore bottoms. "Poor little dears; oh! Miss Coote, you have been cruel to the innocent things."

MISS COOTE.—"How dare you say innocent things when you taught them to steal. I'll make you confess your guilt, you bad woman."

MRS. WHITE, all of a tremble.—"Oh! My heart bleeds for their poor rumps, I can't help what I say."

MISS COOTE.—"Take them away, and let Mary see to their bruises, then come back and help us to cheer up the mother a little; she's dreadfully depressed, poor thing," laughing ironically at Mrs. White.

Jane soon returns, and begins to prepare the mother for her punishment.

MISS COOTE.—"Stretch her properly on the ladder; she's the worst of the lot, first tempting her husband, and then making the children help to steal."

MRS. WHITE.—"Oh! I didn't think you cared about the garden stuff, it would have been spoilt."

MISS COOTE.—"Then why didn't your husband ask me what to do with it? Did you not use the money to buy ribbons and dresses?"

The poor woman groans for very shame, and has nothing to say for herself. Jane and Mademoiselle pull off her bright blue dress, and expose a fine pair of white shoulders, showing that her blushes have extended all down her neck, which is slightly flushed as they uncover it. She is a fine woman with reddish brown hair and hazel eyes, fine plump arms, and hands which do not look as if they worked too hard at home, her underclothing, skirts, and petticoats, although not of the best material, are beautifully white and tastefully trimmed with cheap lace; they soon remove everything, and find her suite *sans culottes* like the little girls; the poor woman blushes scarlet at the exposure of all her luscious-looking charms, her splendid prominent mount being covered with a profusion of long, curly hair, similar to what she has on her head.

MISS COOTE.—"My gracious, Mrs. White, how could you come here for a whipping and have nothing on to cover your modesty; it's shockingly indelicate; what can we do?"

MADEMOISELLE.—"I guessed what would happen; look here, Miss Coote, I amused myself before dinner, and have made her an apron of real fresh vine leaves; how pretty they will look on her, and set off the pink flesh."

The poor woman fairly sobs with shame at our remarks, and laughing jokes about what a fine set of rumpsteaks she has got, and how nicely they will be grilled for her. They adjust the apron of vine leaves very tastefully about her loins, and then present her to me, to kiss the rod, a fine heavy bunch of long, green fresh birchen twigs, tastefully ornamented with gaily coloured ribbons. She is made to kneel, and giving the required kiss, stammer out

as whispered in her ear by Jane. "Oh! Oh! My dear young lady—
Miss Coote—do—do—whip me—soundly—for I have been a
wicked—dishonest woman. Oh! Oh! forgive me, don't be too
hard," she exclaims, forgetting the orders and in a tremble of
anticipation, the tears coursing down her scarlet cheeks, as she
gets upon her feet; and they lay her at full length along the ladder,
which is at a great angle, both arms and feet stretched out as far
as possible, and tied tightly so she can scarcely move her bottom,
or wriggle in the least.

All being in readiness:—

MISS COOTE.—"You have only half confessed your guilt, but
your bottom well warmed will bring you to a full sense of it," as
she waves the tremendous rod about and makes it fairly hiss
through the air, keeping the victim in agitated expectation for
several seconds, when—whack—whack—whack.

Three resounding blows sound through the room, the victim's
bottom immediately shows the result of a confused appearance
of long red marks and weals, whilst the green leaves are flying in
all directions.

MRS. WHITE, screaming in dreadful pain.—"Ah! Oh! Ah—
r—r—re! I can't bear it! Oh! Oh! Spare me, have mercy!" The
muscles of her back and loins showing by their contortions the
agonizing sensations caused by the cuts in her distended and
distressing position.

MISS COOTE.—"How she screams! where's your courage?
why the little girls bore it better than you do; scream away, it
will keep you from thinking too much of the pain, I'm only just
beginning and have not got warm to my work yet," going on
whack—whack—swish—swish, all the while.

VICTIM.—"Oh! Oh! Frightful! Oh! you'll kill me! do have
mercy now."

MISS COOTE.—"You bad woman, will you be a thief again? will
you bring your little ones up to be honest in future? what do you think
of a good birching, does it make your posteriors feel warm?" cutting
blow after blow, with great force and deliberation; the poor woman
is in most excruciating pain, and sobs and moans in her distress.

VICTIM, hysterically.—"Oh! Oh! I know I deserve it. Oh! I will never do it again. Oh! Ah—r—re, how terrible, I feel like being burnt with hot irons!" The blood flows freely from the often bruised weals, and the operator varies her blows so as to inflict the greatest possible torture on the poor woman by cutting her round the loins, making long weals over the lower part of her belly, and stinging the front dreadfully, then across the tender thighs, making the tips of the birch go well in between her legs, causing intense agony.

The fig leaves are all cut off and scattered, making the stems which have been interlaced look like an exploded firework as they still hang about her lacerated loins and buttocks; Miss Coote works herself up into a perfect fury of excitement, and cuts away regardless of the victim's apparent exhaustion, upbraiding her continually and making her promise to take her children to church regularly every Sunday in future, and pay particular attention to the seventh commandment, "Thou shalt not steal."

Mrs. White is almost too far gone to hear half of this objurgation, but slightly moans, "Oh! my God, I shall faint. Let me die in mercy. Thou shalt not steal. My God how I am punished," and fairly swoons under the rod, to the great pleasure of Jane and Mademoiselle, who have exquisitely enjoyed the scene.

The victim is released, when the marks on her wrists and ankles almost cut into the flesh by the tightly tied cords fully attest what she must have suffered from her fearfully stretched position, whilst her bottom and thighs and loins are a perfect pickle of weals and bleeding cuts; the drops of blood quite clotted the beautiful hair on her mount and round the red lips of her "Venus' wrinkle."

Jane and Mary and Polly sponge and relieve the poor woman's soreness, as well as they can, and revive her by plenty of cold water and fresh air, &c., and send her home refreshed by a little more champagne.

Next day, as I was walking the garden with my dear Mademoiselle, we asked White how his wife felt after her whipping, and being a blunt illiterate man he gave us young ladies rather an indelicate answer as follows:—

"I'm darned, Miss, I never had such a night before; I was abed and asleep before she got home with the children, but she was so hot she left them to shift for themselves, and mounted me as you often see the cow do to the bull when she wants him to do his duty; she didn't care how tired I was with my day's work, she was off and on all night. I can't understand her being so on heat, for we always leave that to quiet days like Sundays, but she said it was delightful. Darn me, though, if I liked it quite so much. We shall be having twins, or three or four at once after such a tarnation game as that."

I will send another letter soon, but one thing you must excuse in my rough composition; that is my so often speaking of myself in the third person, which makes it easier to tell my tale.

Yours affectionately,
ROSA BELINDA COOTE.

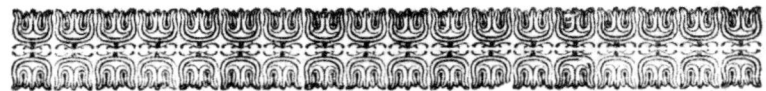

LETTER VII.

My dear Nellie,—

In my last letter you had an account of some pretty everyday larceny, but in this you will read about a pretty young lady who was also a thief by nature, not from any necessity; in fact, it was a case of what they call in these degenerate days Kleptomania; no wonder when downright thieving is called by such an outlandish name that milk-and-water people have almost succeeded in abolishing the good old institution of the rod.

Miss Selina Richards was a cousin of Laura Sandon, my old schoolfellow and first bedfellow at Miss Flaybum's; bye-the-bye, can you explain or did you ever understand how girls can be fellows, but I know of no other term which will apply to the relationship in question. Is there no feminine to that word? It certainly is a defect of the English language.

Well, being on a visit to Laura when I was about eighteen, she mentioned the case to me, saying that her cousin Selina was such an inveterate thief her family were positively afraid to let her go anywhere from home for fear she should get into trouble, and that her parents were obliged to confine her to her room when they had visitors in the house, as the young thief would secrete any trifles, more especially jewelry, she could lay her hands upon, "and you know, Rosa, what an awful disgrace it would be to all the family if she should ever be accused of such a thing."

ROSA.—"But have they never punished her properly, to try and eradicate the vice?"

LAURA.—"They confine her to her room, and often keep the child on bread and water for a week, but all the starving and lecturing in the world won't do any good."

ROSA.—"Have they never tried a good whipping?"

LAURA.—"It never seems to have entered the stupid heads of her father and mother; they are too tender-hearted for anything of that kind."

ROSA.—"Laura, dear, I don't mind confessing to you I should dearly love to birch the little *voleuse;* ever since I left school our last grand séance at the breaking-up party has quite fascinated me—when I think over the beautiful sight of the red bleeding posteriors, the blushes of shame and indignation of the victims, and above all the enjoyment of their distress at being so humiliated and disgraced before others. We often enjoy our old schoolbirchings in private, and a little while ago I administered an awful whipping to our gardener's wife and her two little girls for stealing my fruit, etc., and effected quite a cure, they are strictly honest now. You are coming to see us soon, can't you persuade your uncle and aunt to entrust Selina to your care, with the promise that I am to be thoroughly informed of her evil propensity; on second thoughts I think you should say you have told me, and that I offer to try and cure the girl, if they will only give me a *carte blanche* to punish her in my own way. You will have a great treat, we shall shock the girl's modesty by stripping and exposing her, you will see how delightful the sight of her pretty form is added to the distressing sense of humiliation we will make her feel; the real lovers of the birch watch and enjoy all the expressions of the victim's face, and do all they can to increase the sense of degradation, as well as to inflict terrible and prolonged torture by skilful appliance of the rod, and placing

69

the victim in most painful, distended positions to receive her chastisement."

LAURA.—"What an ogress of cruelty you have become Rosa!"

ROSA, kissing her.—"So will you my dear, with a little more experience, you are much older than me, but really younger in that respect; by judicious use of the rod a club of ladies could enjoy every sensual feeling of pleasure without the society of men. I mean to marry the birch (in fact I am already wedded to it), and retain my fortune as my independence."

LAURA.—"What a paragon of virtue, do I really understand you pander to your sensuality without intercourse with men?"

ROSA.—"Come and see, that is my only answer to such a dear sceptic, only manage to bring the pretty *voleuse* with you, and you will have every reason to be satisfied with your visit."

Laura was quite successful in her application to the parents of Selina; they thought the visit might perhaps result in some good to their daughter, and readily gave all the required assurances as to liberty of inflicting punishment for any little dishonesty we might detect.

On their arrival at our house Selina was allotted a small room to herself, whilst Laura asked and was allowed to be my bedfellow again. Nothing was put out of the way, as I was so thoroughly assured of the honesty of all about me, and felt certain that if Miss Selina did steal anything, she could only secrete it and would have no opportunity to dispose of the plunder, so we might be sure to recover all our lost property.

Miss Richards had received a very careful education, and, in general, was a most interesting young lady, and apparently very modest and retiring.

Several days passed very pleasantly, and it almost seemed as if Missie's fingers had forgot their cunning. I was just beginning to fear we might lose our victim for want of a fair opportunity, but it turned out to be only a kind of natural shyness, which would disappear when she found herself quite at home.

Things began to vanish, my jewelry seemed much preferred, first a small diamond ring, then an opal brooch set with pearls, gloves, scarfs, and any small articles walked off mysteriously, but no one could ever detect her even setting her foot in my room in the day time, and so Laura and I determined to watch at night. We usually went into Selina's room the last thing before retiring ourselves, when her eyes were invariably closed.

Our resolve was put in practice the first night, and about two hours after we were supposed to be safely asleep, the creaking hinge of the door gave us a slight admonition of the stealthy approach of someone.

We could hear no footstep, but caught a glimpse of Miss Prig putting her head just inside the door to see all was right.

We were motionless, our heads being well within the shade of the bed curtains, whilst a dim moonlight partially lighted up the rest of the chamber. The little *voleuse,* as stealthily as a Red Indian, actually crawled on her hands and knees to the dressing table, and then without raising her body, groped with her hand on the top of the table for anything that might be lying about; in fact, we could see nothing of her as we were in bed, but could plainly hear the slight movement of the articles as they were touched or moved.

Off went the bedclothes, with a cry, "Now we have her safe, the sly thief." I sprang to the door and cut off her retreat, whilst Laura acted the policeman, by sternly arresting the confused prisoner.

Turning the key in the lock, we at once laid her over the foot of our bed, with her feet resting on the floor, and turning up her nightdress, administered with our hands a good slapping till she fairly screamed for mercy.

"Oh! Oh! Pray, Miss Coote, forgive me. Let me go, I won't come here again. Oh! Ah—r—r—re! Indeed I won't," struggling and writhing under our smarting slaps. We could see even by the faint light how red her bottom was, and at last we released her with the assurance of a full enquiry next day, and advised her to give up all she had stolen or it would be worse for her.

By my orders, she was confined to her room in the morning, and Jane acted as gaoler. After dinner, about six o'clock, she brought the prisoner before me in the punishment room.

To make my proceedings more impressive, all the establishment were present, except Charlie the page, who being masculine, I did not think it would be decent to have him admitted.

MISS COOTE.—"Selina Richards, you stand before me a convicted thief caught in the act. Have you restored all your booty, you sly young cat?"

SELINA (with a crimson face and downcast eyes).—"Oh! Oh! I have indeed, ask Jane, she has searched the room and can't find any more but what I gave up to her. Ah! Miss Coote, I don't know how I could have done it; I'm so ashamed of myself and sorry to have been so wicked. Oh! Oh! What shall I do?" quite overcome and bursting into tears.

JANE.—"If you please Miss, I've got everything but your ring, that I can't find anywhere."

MISS COOTE.—"You bad girl, I know your character; don't think you can deceive me by your feigned tears and repentance. What have you done with my ring, eh?"

SELINA (appealing in great and apparently genuine distress and consternation).—"Oh! I have never seen it. Indeed, I didn't take that, Miss Coote. Ah, you must believe me, I am so degraded to feel how guilty I am. I had the brooch, but have given that and everything else up to Jane."

MISS COOTE.—"I don't believe what you say about the ring, and will birch you well till you really confess the truth. Now strip the little thief, and examine every article of clothing as it is taken off. Shake out all the braids of her hair, she may have it there."

Notwithstanding her confusion, I noticed a slight gleam of satisfaction pass across her countenance, for which, at the time, I was puzzled to account.

They proceeded with the undressing, and I could not help noticing her continued satisfaction as each garment was over-hauled, as much as to say, "You haven't found it yet," which convinced me she had the ring very cunningly secreted somewhere, but for the life of me, I was quite at a loss to think how she could have disposed of it, as Jane assured me there was not a chink in her room where it could possibly be put, she had even ripped up the bed in her search.

At last they let down all the braids of her hair, and she stood in her chemise, blushing crimson at the exposure, her usually damask cheeks as rosy as ripe cherries. She evidently now considered the search at an end, as she kicked off the drawers and protested against my order to "remove the last rag."

"Oh! Oh! Pray don't expose me, there can't be anything in that."

MISS COOTE.—"But there may be somewhere else."

The suddenly abashed look that came over her face convinced me I was now getting near a discovery. Her legs were closely nipped together, and she covered her hairless mount with her hands.

MISS COOTE.—"Give me a birch Jane, I'll make her jump," then taking the switch in hand cuts smartly over Miss Selina's knuckles, "remove your hands, Miss Prig, now jump will you," repeating the blow on the naked bottom with such effect that the poor girl screamed with pain, but still kept her legs close; again the rod descended with a terrific undercut, "won't you open your legs and jump Miss." This time it was effective; with a fearful scream the victim threw herself down on the carpet, but she was unable to prevent the escape of the ring which rolled out on the floor.

It would be impossible to describe the poor girl's distress and confusion now her guilt was so thoroughly established; she was crimson all over, and tried to hide her face in her hands as she cried for shame; her bottom had some fine looking red marks, and also in between her thighs, which the last cut had inflicted.

MISS COOTE.—"Look at the little thief, she thinks to hide herself by covering her face, she doesn't care about exposing all her private parts, or using them to hide my ring, what a disgustingly clever trick; Jane, put on her chemise and drawers; if she does not care I do, and like to do birching decently with all propriety."

Jane and Polly lift her up, and put on the required articles, then as she stands before me still sobbing with shame and pain, I had never seen a more delicious looking victim; she had such a beautiful brunette complexion, her almost black hair hanging all down her back to her loins, pretty white rounded globes with dark brown nipples looked impudently above her chemisette, which only reached a little way down her thighs; it was tastefully trimmed with lace all round, and seemed to draw attention to her beautiful thighs and legs, the latter set off by blue silk stockings with handsome garters and lovely boots.

Jane whispers in the culprit's ears, and Selina humbly kneels before me, saying in broken accents:—

"Oh! how can I speak to you, dear Miss Coote. I—I—have so disgraced—myself. Will—will—you ever forgive me. Oh! What shall I do—will you punish me properly and cut—the—the—awful propensity out of me—indeed, dear Miss Coote—I can't help myself—my fingers—my fingers will take the things—even—when I don't—want them," as she kisses the rod and bursts into a torrent of hysterical tears.

By my orders the victim is well stretched out on the ladder, as I generally preferred it to the whipping post, and having armed myself with a very light rod made of fine pieces of whalebone, which would sting awfully without doing serious damage, I went up to the ladder for a commencement, but first made them loosen her a bit, and place a thick sofa bolster under her loins, then fasten her tightly again with her bottom well presented, the drawers pinned back on each side, and her chemise rolled up and secured under her arms; poor Selina seemed to know well enough what was coming, it checked her tears, but she begged and screamed piteously for me to forgive and wait and see if she ever stole anything again.

MISS COOTE, laughing.—"Why what a little coward you are. I should have thought such a bold thief would have more spirit, and I have hardly touched you yet; you won't be hurt more than you can fairly bear; you would do it again directly if I don't beat it out of you now."

SELINA.—"My arms and limbs are so dreadfully stretched,

and my poor behind still smarts from the three whacks you gave. Oh! Have pity! Have mercy! Dear Miss Coote."

MISS COOTE.—"I must not listen to such childish nonsense, you're both a thief and a dreadful liar, Miss Selina, will you—will you—do it again," giving three smart stinging cuts, the whalebone fairly hissing through the air as she flourishes it before each stroke to make it sound more effective.

SELINA.—"Ah! Ah! Ah—r—r—re! I can't bear it, you're thrashing me with wires, the blows are red hot. Oh! Oh! I'll never, never do it again!" her bottom finely streaked already with thin red lines, the painful agony being greatly increased by the strain on her wrists and ankles as she cannot restrain her writhing at each cut.

MISS COOTE.—"You don't seem to like it, Selina, but indeed it's for your good, how would you like to be branded B. C. with a really red hot iron, you'd sing a still different tune then; but I'm wasting my time—there—there—there—you've only had six yet, how you do howl you silly girl!"

SELINA.—"Ah—r—r—r—re!" with a prolonged shriek. "You're killing me. Oh! I shall soon die!" her bottom redder than ever.

MISS COOTE.—"You'll have a dozen whalebone cuts," counting and cutting deliberately till she calls twelve, then giving a little pause as if finished; she lets the victim compose the features with a sigh of relief, and just then gives another thundering whack, exclaiming, "Ah! Ha! Ha! Ha! you thought I had done, did you, Miss Prig; it was a baker's dozen you were to get, I always give thirteen as twelve for fear of having missed one, and like to give the last just as they think it is all over."

SELINA.—"I know it's well deserved, but oh! so cruel, you will let me go now; pray forgive me, indeed, you may depend upon me in the future," still sighing and quivering from the effects of the last blow.

MISS COOTE.—"You're not to get off so easily, Miss Prig, your bottom would be all right in a few minutes, and then you would only laugh when you think of it. The real rod is to come, look at this bum-tickler, it's the real birch grown in my own grounds, and well pickled in brine these last two days, to be ready for you when caught. It will bring your crime to mind in a more awful light, and leave marks to make you remember it for days to come."

SELINA.—"Pray let me have a drink, if I must suffer so much more, my tongue is as dry as a board, Miss Coote, you are cruel, I am not old enough to bear such torture."

MISS COOTE.—"Be quiet, you shall have a drink of champagne, but don't talk about your tender age, that makes your crime still worse, for you have shown such precocious disgusting cunning, far beyond your years."

She has the refreshing draught and the rod resumes its sway.

MISS COOTE.—"You bad girl, your bottom shall be marked for many a day; I'll wager you don't steal as long as the marks remain. Two dozen's the punishment, and then we'll see to your bruises, and put you to bed. One—two—three—four," increasing the force of the blows scientifically with each cut, and soon beginning to draw the skin up into big bursting blood-red weals.

VICTIM.—"Mother! Mother! Ah! Ah—r—r—re! I shall die. Oh! kill me quickly, if you won't have mercy." She writhes in such agony that her muscles stand out like whipcord, and by their continued quivering, straining action, testify to the intensity of her pain.

MISS COOTE, laughing and getting excited.—"That's right, call your mother, she'll soon help you. Ha! Ha! She didn't think how I should cure you, when your papa gave his consent for me to punish you as I like. Five, six, seven," she goes on counting and thrashing the poor girl over the back, ribs, loins, and thighs, wealing her everywhere, as well as on the posteriors. All the spectators are greatly moved, and seem to enjoy the sight of Selina's blood dripping down, down till her stockings are saturated and it forms little pools beneath her on the floor.

The victim has not sufficient strength to stand this very long, her head droops, and she is too weak to scream, moaning and sighing fainter and fainter, till at last she fairly swoons, and the rod is stopped at the twenty-second stroke.

Miss Coote is quite exhausted with her exertions, and sinking on a sofa, fondly embraces her friend Laura, describing to her all the thrilling sensations she has enjoyed during the operation, which the flushed cheeks and sparkling soft large blue eyes of Laura show she is beginning to duly appreciate.

Mademoiselle Fosse and the servants lay Selina on the floor, and sprinkle her face with water, whilst one of them uses a very large fan most effectively; her lacerated bottom is sponged with strong salt and water, and she soon shows signs of regaining animation. Sighing and sobbing, "Where, where am I? Oh! I remember, Miss Coote's cut my bottom off. Oh! Oh! Ah! How it smarts and burns!" They pour a little liqueur down her throat, and she is soon quite conscious again, and cries quite hysterically over her pickled state.

MADEMOISELLE.—"Now for the finishing touch. Mary, fetch that pot from the kitchen, and bring the bag of feathers."

SELINA (piteously).—"Oh, haven't you done yet? What have I to suffer?" wringing her hands in apprehension.

MADEMOISELLE.—"Here it is. We won't keep you in suspense," taking the brush from a pot of warm tar, held by Mary. "This will heal your bruises, and prevent the flies getting at your sore bottom, this warm weather."

They make her stand up, and Mademoiselle paints all over her posteriors, and the lower part of her belly inside her thighs, and even the crack of her bottom, with the hot stuff, regardless of the great pain she is inflicting.

SELINA (shrieking in fearful distress and shame at this degradation).—"Ah! This is worse than all, you're actually scalding me; my skin will peel off," dancing about in excruciating agony.

MADEMOISELLE (laughing).—"My dear, it is to heal and keep your skin on. We're going to cover you with nice warm feathers. You never felt so comfortable in your life as you will presently."

The ceremony was both amusing and exciting, but it would be impossible to describe the poor girl's misery and dreadful shame. Her shrieks and appeals of "Oh! Ah! It will never come off," especially as they lift her up and roll her bottom and front in a great heap of feathers, taking care to shove them in everywhere, so as to thoroughly cover all the tar.

This is the finale, and she is led from the scene of her punishment and degradation; but that was not all; every day for nearly three weeks she had to strip and exhibit her feathery bum for inspection and laughing remarks. I need scarcely say the ordeal she went through effected a radical cure of the Kleptomania.

Do you not think, dear Nellie, my plan would cure the Kleptomaniacs of the present day? It would be well worth a trial.

Yours affectionately,
ROSA BELINDA COOTE.

LETTER VIII.

My Dear Nellie,

I do not intend to trouble you with all the little incidents of domestic discipline which my strict regulations so often brought under notice, and required the exercise of the beloved rod, but only write out for your amusement a few of my most remarkable recollections.

The cure of Selina Richards brought me very considerable fame amongst a large circle of acquaintances and friends, but I steadily refused to take charge of my more *mauvais sujets*, but devoted myself to promoting a Ladies Club exclusively for the admirers of Birch Discipline. The meetings were to be held at my house, where my servants would be sworn to secrecy, and to act as sub-members, not on an equality with the ladies of our Club.

The rules specially enjoined secrecy on every member, so that novices might not obtain the slightest inkling of the ordeal they would have to undergo when initiated into the mysteries of Lady Rodney's Club, as it was called, our object being to make our séances for the receiving of new members the means of affording us the most exquisite enjoyment, by bringing out all their modest bashfulness, and studying their distress and horror at finding themselves stripped and exposed for flagellation before all the sisters of the rod.

My old schoolfellows, Laura Sandon, Louise Van Tromp, Hon. Miss Cecile Deben, Lady Clara Wavering, and three other ladies besides Mdlle. Fosse and myself, as president and manager, were the first members; two of them were married, but we agreed that everyone should be known to the other sisters by her maiden name only.

Lady Clara was the first to propose a novice for admission to the Club; it was a younger sister of hers, who she informed us had a great penchant for young gentlemen, having several times seriously misconducted herself with youthful friends of the opposite sex, so that her lecture and castigation would be of a most piquant description.

We fixed an evening for her introduction, and were all present to inaugurate the Club's first séance of admission.

Our large punishment room was tastefully draped all around with elegant curtains, and brilliantly illuminated by clusters of wax candles projecting from the walls, above handsome mirrors set in bouquets of lovely flowers.

The ladies of the Club were all dressed in the same costume, viz., blue silk corsets with scarlet silk laces, and short skirts of white tulle, only coming a little below the knee, so as to show all the beautiful legs in pink silk stockings and high-heeled Parisian boots. All were in these short skirts, the outer dresses being discarded to allow a greater freedom of action, and also display for the glorious necks and bosoms of the members, who were every one young and beautiful, flushed with excitement and anticipation, their snow-white globes heaving at each breath, and set off to the greatest advantage by bouquets of red roses adjusted between the lovely hillocks of love.

As president, I was seated in a chair of state, supported on either side by four ladies, whilst Jane and Mary stand behind me.

A knock at the door; Lady Clara advances to open it, and introduces her sister, Lady Lucretia Wavering, about sixteen, but otherwise a very counterpart of herself, dark, well proportioned, rather above the medium height, languid expression, and large pensive hazel eyes. She holds a beautiful bouquet in one hand, and is dressed in simple white.

Advancing right up to where I was seated, she makes a profound bow, and Lady Clara says, "Permit me, Miss President and ladies of the Lady Rodney Club, to introduce to you my sister, Lady Lucretia, who is desirous of being admitted a member."

PRESIDENT.—"Lady Lucretia, we welcome you to our sisterhood. Are you willing to take the oaths of secrecy, and be initiated into the mysteries of the rod?"

LADY LUCRETIA.—"Yes, and to be submissive to all your rules and regulations."

PRESIDENT.—"You must now strip and assume the costume of a member, and must truthfully answer any questions I may put to you."

Jane and Mary as servants assist to disrobe the novice, who blushes slightly as they proceed to remove her skirts after taking away her dress.

LUCRETIA, turning to me.—"You surely don't strip us quite naked, I thought I had only to change the dress."

PRESIDENT.—"Yes, everything, because you have to taste the birch before assuming our costume."

LUCRETIA, blushing deeply.—"Ah! Oh! I never expected that, it's so indecent."

PRESIDENT.—"Make haste, such improper remarks must be checked; Sister Lucretia, you have already broken the rules by objecting to lawful orders, your bottom shall smart soundly for it."

LUCRETIA, in great confusion and faltering voice.—"Pray permit me to apologize, I had no idea the members were liable to chastisement, but thought they amused themselves whipping charity children sent up by schools for punishment."

PRESIDENT.—"You will have to do that under the rod; we are quite above tickling the bottoms of school children here, although it is the duty of every member to exercise proper discipline in any house or place where she may have authority."

81

Lucretia is silent, but the scarlet face and nervous twichings of the corners of her mouth attest how she feels about the approaching taste of the rod; her eyes are cast down in shame, and presently with nothing but her drawers, chemise, boots, and stockings on, they lead her to the ladder, the president and ladies all rising and clustering round the victim.

PRESIDENT.—"Have the ladder nearly upright, with her wrists secured high up, and let her toes only just touch the floor; woe to her bum if she dares to step on the bottom rung of the ladder without orders."

The victim with tears of shame and apprehension protests against this disposition of her body as being too painful, and cries out for mercy as she feels her chemise rolled up and fastened under her armpits, and her unbuttoned drawers pulled down to her knees. "Ah! Ah! Oh! You'll never be so bad as that to a novice! Oh! have mercy, dear Miss Coote."

PRESIDENT.—"Don't show the white feather, young lady; we're going to initiate you into a most delightful society. You will soon be one of the most active of the sisterhood," taking from Jane a very elegantly tied-up rod, ornamented with blue and gold ribbons, then just lightly switching the victim's bare bottom, "Now ask me to birch you properly, and beg pardon for your frivolous objections."

LUCRETIA, in a tremor of fear, and with faltering voice.— "Oh! is there no getting off; why must I be cruelly whipped?"

PRESIDENT, with a smart cut across her beautiful buttocks, which at once brings the roses to the surface.—"There, that's a slight taste, you stupid, obstinate girl, I can't waste more time, there, there, there," giving three more sharp cuts in succession, each leaving their respective long red marks. "Perhaps in a minute or two you will think it worth while to obey orders, and beg pardon, &c."

VICTIM.—"Ah! Ah—r—r—re! it is cruel, oh! oh! I am sorry for saying so! the cuts smart so it's impossible to think what one's saying. Oh! pray forgive me, and punish me properly. But—but—oh! be merciful!" as she writhes and wriggles under the painful strokes which already begin to weal her delicate, tender skin.

PRESIDENT.—"Very well, you've done it after a fashion; but now as you're becoming one of our members, pray have you got a sweetheart?"

VICTIM, just then receiving an extra sharp cut.—"Ah—r—r—r—re! Oh! oh! I can't bear it, it's like a hot knife cutting the skin! Indeed, I have not got a lover, if that's not allowed!" putting her feet on the rungs of the ladder to ease the painful strain on her wrists.

PRESIDENT, with a tremendous whack across the calves of the legs, which makes Miss Lucretia fairly spring with agony.— "How dare you alter my disposition of your body by putting your feet on the ladder?" switching her legs again and again with great heavy cuts, till the poor girl capers like a cat on hot bricks. "Perhaps you won't do that again, but wait till I give you the order presently. Now about lovers, of course you have had one, if not just at present?"

LUCRETIA, in smarting pain.—"On! Oh! My poor legs! Oh! Yes! Ah—r—r—re! But I gave him up six months ago. Have mercy, or how can I speak to answer your questions?"

PRESIDENT, without relaxing her smarting strokes.—"Out of order again, Sister Lucretia. Your rosy-looking bottom must be enjoying the fun, or you would never keep questioning my discretion as you do. How do you like it? Does it smart very much? Tell us a little more about your lover, if you please."

LUCRETIA, writhing in agony.—"My wrists are breaking, and my bottom—oh! my bottom burns and smarts so! Ah! You want to know about my lover. I gave him up because—because he behaved improperly to me."

PRESIDENT.—"Are you speaking the truth, Sister Lucretia? as that is a most essential thing with us. We call the birch the Rod of Truth, for it is sure to bring everything out. What did he do to you? Cry out if you are in great pain, we like to hear it, and it will do you good."

LUCRETIA.—"Ah, indeed! I must shriek! You cut me so

83

dreadfully. Oh! He took liberties with me, and put his hands up my clothes, that's all. Ah! Have mercy! You don't give time for me to get my breath."

PRESIDENT.—"Are you sure that's not a bit of a fib?" slackening a little with the rod.

LUCRETIA, thinking she is now going to be let off.—"It's quite true, my dear Miss Coote, that's what he did," and beginning to feel a deliciously voluptuous warmth and lubricity in her sensitive parts, she shut her eyes, whilst a sensuous smile betrays her pleasurable emotions.

PRESIDENT.—"What are you thinking of, Sister Lucretia, with that satisfied smile? How your buttocks seem to quiver with some curious emotion. Has my question about your lover revived anything in your mind of past enjoyments. Out with the truth. I believe you have been telling a lot of fibs," cutting the astonished victim in a terrible rage with a perfect shower of blows, which weal and bring blood for the first time.

VICTIM.—"Oh! Oh! Ah! Ah! How cruel! Just as I thought it was all over, and began to feel a delicious warmth in my posteriors. Indeed, I was not thinking of my lover," casting down her eyes, and blushing more than ever in a very confused manner.

PRESIDENT, sternly.—"How dare you persist in telling so many fibs. We happen to know a little of your goings on with young Aubrey. Speak the truth at once, or I will cut your impudent bottom into ribbons of scarified flesh. You can't deceive us, we know the effects of the rod, and the voluptuous feelings it induces." All the while, whack—whack—whack sound the blows of the birch, as they ruthlessly cut and weal the victim's bottom. The operator gets quite excited, and feels all the thrilling sensation; each stroke has an electrical effect on her nerves; the cries and screams of Lucretia seem most delightful to her, and all the spectators are in ecstasies of voluptuous emotions. The victim fairly shrieks in agony, she writhes her body about, displaying her lovely figure in a variety of contortions, shifting continually at every scathing touch of the birch.

The ladies at first watched the scene with rapt attention, but gradually the blood courses in warm excitement through their veins, mantling their cheeks with a flesh-like bloom; their eyes sparkle with unusual animation, and at last, by a common impulse the eight ladies, with Jane and Mary, each take a fine long light rod of green twigs; they form a circle round the President as she continues to flagellate the victim on the ladder; each raises her skirts under her arms so as to leave all exposed from the waist downwards. For a moment there is a lovely scene of plump white buttocks and thighs, fascinating legs encased in silk stockings, pretty garters and attractive elegant shoes, set off with jewelled buckles, and, above all, such an inviting collection of impudent looking cunnies, ornamented with every shade of chevelure, black, auburn, or light brown; then all is motion, the birch rods soon put a rosy polish on the pretty bums, each one doing her best to repay on the bottom in front of her the smarting cuts she feels behind. Laughter, shrieks, and ejaculations fill the apartment, and their motions are so rapid as to make quite a rainbow of excited peris round the central figures; but this luscious scene only lasts three or four minutes; the victim, under the President's rod, gets exhausted, her shrieks sink into sobs, and at last she sighs lower and lower, then fairly faints, with her head hanging helplessly back, and her limp form a picture of weals and blood, which oozes from the cuts, and slowly trickles down the white flesh of her thighs.

PRESIDENT, throwing aside her broken and used-up rod.— "There ladies, stop your game and all help to bring her round, she'll soon recover; how pretty your rosy bottoms look, I shall join in the next ring that is formed."

The victim is loosed from the ladder, and by use of a large fan, Lucretia soon shows signs of returning animation, her eyes open, and she looks around in bewilderment. "Where am I? What a beautiful dream!" she murmurs in a low voice, then a little more refreshed by a strong cordial poured down her throat, "Ah! I remember, my bottom smarts so!" Putting her hand down to feel her posteriors she looks at the blood which stains her fingers, and sobs hysterically, "What a cruel girl that Miss Coote must

85

be, and how she seemed to gloat over my sufferings. Ah! let me only handle the tickler over her bum someday."

At this we all burst out into a loud laugh, and thoroughly enjoyed poor Lucretia's shame and confusion.

MISS COOTE.—"Cheer up, Sister Lucretia, you have only to do what we call stepping the ladder, someday you will have a chance of revenge, but you will find Louise Van Tromp quite as cruel as I am, when she uses the birch in her skilful style on your half-cooked bum. Come Jane, I think she is ready for the second edition of her punishment."

LOUISE VAN TROMP.—"Ah! trust me, Sister Rosa, to do my duty, she has not half confessed to us yet," taking up and switching a fine birch rod, making it fairly hiss through the air, to the evident terror of the victim.

LUCRETIA, with sobs and tears running in streams down her cheeks.—"Oh! Oh! how horrible, will you never have mercy; my bottom is so sore I really can't bear it to be touched," shrinking back as Jane tries to draw her to the ladder. "Oh! No! Not again on that awful thing!"

Louise brings down her rod with a tremendous whack across the poor girl's bare shoulders, exclaiming, "What are you hanging back for, look sharp, quick, or I'll cut your shoulders again," looking with delight on the red marks her cut has left on the white flesh of the victim.

LUCRETIA.—"Oh! Oh! I will! I will!" holding up her wrists for Jane to secure them, which is quickly done.

LOUISE.—"Now, step on the rungs of the ladder one at a time, as I call out the number beginning at the bottom, if you take two at once you must do it over again. Now, one"—giving a terrible whack on the victim's bruised rump.

"Ah—r—r—r—re!" shrieks Lucretia, in terrible agony as the birch cuts into the already lacerated skin, but careful only to take one step.

LOUISE, making her birch flourish through the air with a hissing noise.—"Pretty well, now—now—now," keeping her in trembling suspense. "Two—three," giving a couple of crashing strokes with a good interval between them, to make the victim feel the effect as much as possible.

Lucretia gives a fearful shriek at each cut, and sobs out hysterically, "Ah! How dreadful, the skin of my bottom will burst, it's getting so tight."

LOUISE.—"Glad you enjoy it so, dear, I'm sorry to hurt you much," looking delightedly round at the other members. "Now—now—now—"—with another flourish—"four—five," each blow draws the blood afresh from the already crimsoned surface, and puts the spectators into a flutter of excitement.

Lucretia fairly groans, but only once makes a false step, which she corrects before Louise can find fault. "Only two more," she sighs, as if calculating the steps yet to be done.

LOUISE.—"Steady, keep your bottom well out," switching her lightly underneath so as to tickle the exposed pussey, then another grand flourish. "Six—seven," these are awful crackers, but the victim keeps herself steady, and her pluck is greeted by clapping of hands all round. Jane takes advantage of the opportunity to secure the victim's ankles so that she is fixed in a most inviting attitude for further flagellation.

LOUISE.—"Thanks, Jane, very thoughtful of you. Now, Sister Lucretia, before you are let off you must tell us all about yourself and young Aubrey. Miss Coote did not half get it out of you," whisking the tightly bent bottom in a playful way with her rod, but the victim is evidently so sore that even light strokes make twinges of pain pass across her scarlet face.

LUCRETIA.—"Oh! Oh! Pray don't begin again. I told you he took liberties with me, what more can I say? Oh! Oh! Don't touch me; the least whisk of that thing gives awful pain."

LOUISE.—"Then, you silly girl, why do you persist in keeping back the truth? Did you not encourage him?" making the victim writhe under her painful touches, which, although not very heavy, seem to have great effect on the raw bottom, in such a tightly bent position.

LUCRETIA, in great shame and confusion, and seeming to crimson all over at the thoughts of her degradation before them all.—"Oh! Oh! Spare me! If you know all, have mercy, consider my feelings, how painful such a confession must be. Ah—r—r—rre! You are shameful girls to enjoy my pain and shame so," sobbing as if her heart would break.

LOUISE.—"Come! Come! It is not so bad as that. Make a clean breast and be one of us in future. You will enjoy such scenes yourself when the next novice is admitted; but I can't play with you. There—there—there!" cutting three brisk strokes on the bent bottom.

LUCRETIA.—"Ah! Oh! Oh! I shall faint again. It's like burning with red hot irons. Ah! You know he seduced me, and—I must confess I did not resist as I ought. Something tempted me to taste the sweets of love, and your President's birching brought all the thrilling sensations back to me, and when I fainted my dream was all about the bliss enjoyed in my lover's arms."

LOUISE, still lightly using her rod.—"A little better, and getting nearer the truth, but you still prevaricate, so in trying to excuse your own fault. Now, did you not seduce the youth instead of his taking advantage of you?"

LUCRETIA.—"Oh! Pity me. I saw him lying asleep on the grass in a secluded part of the garden; he was so sleepy that I failed to wake him, but I since believe he was shamming. Noticing a lump of something in his breeches, I gently pressed it with my fingers to see what it was, when it gradually swelled under my pressure and became like a hard stick throbbing under the cloth; my blood was fired; I can't tell how I did it, but presently, when he opened his eyes and laughed at me, I found myself with his exposed shaft in my hand. He jumped up, sprang upon me, and taking advantage of my confusion, I own he had an easy conquest. But something of the sort will happen to every loving girl at some time or other. Now I have told you all, have pity and let me go," sobbing and looking dreadfully confused and distressed.

She was let down, and we all crowded round her, giving affectionate kisses and welcoming her to be a real sister of Lady Rodney's Club.

The poor girl was very sore, and sobbed over her poor bruised bottom. "Oh! Oh! I can't sit down, it will be weeks before I can do anything with comfort. Ah! You pretend to be kind now after all that dreadful cruelty. I only wish we could get Aubrey and give him a good thrashing, it would do the impetuous boy good." We had another laugh at this, but assured her our rules didn't provide for admitting any of the opposite sex to the séances of the Club; but in my next you shall see what happened, and how Lucretia tricked us by introducing young Aubrey as a young lady novice desirous of admission to our Society. I remain, dear Nellie,

Yours affectionately,
—ROSA BELINDA COOTE.

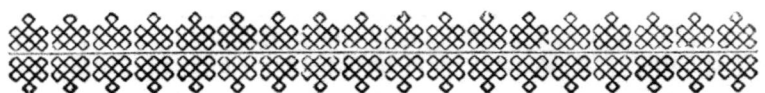

LETTER IX.

———

My dear Nellie,—

I have been looking over some of my grandfather's papers, and found the following curious little bit written by his brother Dean Coote, "Remarks on the influence of Female Beauty":—

I shall reverse the general practice, and instead of beginning with the head, commence with the leg, and hope to get credit for so doing. A pretty face, sparkling eyes, rosy cheeks, delicate complexion, smiles, dimples, hair dark, auburn or blonde, have all, it is acknowledged, great weight in the business of love; but still let me appeal to every impartial and unprejudiced observer, which he is most curious to behold, the legs or the face of his favourite lady.

Whether does the face or the legs of a pretty girl that is clambering over a style, or mounting a ladder, most attract our notice and regard?

What is it that causes my lord to smack his chops in that wanton lecherous manner, as he is sauntering up and down the lounge in Bond Street, with his glass in hand, to watch the ladies getting in and out of their carriages? And what is it that draws together such vast crowds of the holiday gentry at Easter and Whitsuntide, to see the merry rose-faced lasses running down the hill in Greenwich Park?

What is it causes such a roar of laughter and applause when a merry girl happens to overset in her career, and kick her heels in the air?

Lastly, as the parsons all say, what is it that makes the theatrical ballets so popular?

It has frequently been remarked by travellers that in no nation of the world are the ladies more nice and curious about their legs than in England; and to do them justice there is perhaps no nation in the world where the ladies have greater reason to show them like pretty girls in dirty weather, when the fear of passing for dragtails causes the pretty creatures to hold their petticoats up behind, and display their lovely calves and ankles above par. But I am infinitely more delighted with my muddy walk than were I making an excursion in the finest sunshiny day imaginable. There is a kind of magic in the sight of a handsome female leg, which is not in the power of language to describe, to be conceived it must be felt.

We read in the memoirs of Brantôme of a certain illustrious lady, who was so fully sensible of the vast importance of a handsome leg that once having the misfortune to break one of hers by a fall from a horse, and the surgeon by some inadvertency or other, failing to set the bone straight, she was so grieved at this accident that she actually had the fortitude to snap it across a second time on purpose and with design, then sending for a more skilful doctor, took care to have her leg carefully reset, by which means it was restored to its former grace and loveliness.

Some of my readers may, perhaps, condemn this conduct in the lady; for my part, I cannot but greatly admire both the soundness of her judgment and the amazing strength of her mind. But too well am I acquainted, from experience, with the magic which centres in a pretty leg, a delicate ankle, and well-proportioned calf.

The first time that I was in love (I perfectly well remember the circumstances as if it occurred but yesterday), the first time I could ever be said to feel what love is, I had to thank a pretty leg for it. I was then in my teens, as harmless and innocent a young fellow as needs be. My friends were of the strictest sect of religion. I was nolens volens brought up in their principles. Plays, novels, and all kinds of books which treat upon the subject of love were denied me; my parents were ambitious that I should be a second Joseph, and had partly succeeded in this pious design, when, lo! one single unlucky circumstance completely baffled all their endeavours.

It was a beautiful summer's day. I had strolled into the wood, laying myself down in a copse of young hazel trees, and alternately musing and dozing away, when my curiosity was excited by a rustling noise close to the spot where I lay concealed. I was all attention; and directing my inquisitive eyes to the quarter from whence the noise proceeded, discovered a lovely rosy-cheeked girl, who lay basking, as it were, in the sun, and deeming herself sufficiently remote from observation, was under no restraint in her motions. Presently up she whips her coats and ungarters her stockings, contemplates her legs, turns them this way, and that way, and in short practised a thousand manœuvers, which I have not at present leisure to expatiate upon; suffice it to say not a single movement was lost upon me, and from that hour to the present moment, I never see a pretty leg but I feel certain unutterable emotions within me, which seem to realize the observations of the poet:—

> Should some fair youth, the charming sight explore,
> In rapture lost he'll gaze, and wish for something more!

The Dean was quite right in his pretty delicate remarks about the influence of the leg; although only a woman, the same magic influence affects me; when I see a pretty pair of calves in silk stockings it makes me long to look higher, and have the bottom which belongs to them under a nice birch rod.

To return to my experiences, novices were rather shy of offering themselves as candidates for admission to Lady Rodney's Club, but one day, two or three weeks after the séance described in my last, Lucretia called upon me, apparently very much excited, and her errand was to tell me that Maria Aubrey, the sister of her quondam lover, wished to join us, and asked me to fix a day for her admission.

Knowing the young lady to be a very desirable subject, and to belong to a most aristocratic family, I could make no objections, and expressed my pleasure at the acquisition I hoped she would prove to the sisterhood, and appointed that day week for the reception of the novice.

When I mentioned the proposal to Lady Clara and asked what she knew of the young lady, she assured me that she had not yet the pleasure of her acquaintance as the young lady had been at school in Germany for some years, and was only just returned home.

Lucretia kept away from me till the eventful evening, but arrived punctually at seven o'clock with her protégée, who appeared slightly taller than herself, rather slim, with blue eyes, and dressed in white for the occasion; in fact, she seemed a very quiet, good-looking girl, the only thing specially attractive about her being a remarkable merry twinkle of her eyes, which seemed to look everywhere, and enjoy the sight of everything.

We were all present, and myself as usual seated as President, surrounded by the others. Lady Lucretia presented the novice without delay, taking her by the hand and leading her close up to the chair, then bowing, says, "Allow me, dear Miss Coote and sisters of Lady Rodney's Club, to present to you Miss Maria Aubrey, a dear friend of mine, who wishes to be admitted to your society."

PRESIDENT.—"Miss Maria Aubrey, are you willing to submit to our initiative ordeal and swear to obey the rules enacted by a majority of the members?"

MARIA.—"Yes, I am anxious to be admitted, we had so much of the birch in Germany, that I am an enthusiast in the use of the rod."

PRESIDENT.—"Let her be sworn as usual," after which she resumes, "Now Sister Maria, you will have to strip and assume the regular costume which we have provided for you."

The novice blushed deeply, and seemed quite at a loss what to say, and I noticed that Lucretia was hugely enjoying the scene. From some secret cause she whispered something to Lady Clara, and the latter to Mdlle. Fosse, who imparted the information to me "that our novice was not in reality Maria Aubrey, but her brother Frank, Lucretia's lover, whom she had persuaded to personate his sister, without in the least letting him know what he would have to go through, and no doubt was quite nonplussed at the idea of being stripped and exposed."

I must confess that I felt quite a flush of anger at learning the trick Lucretia had put upon all of us, but by the whispered advice of Mdlle. Fosse I proceeded as if nothing was known. "Come Sister Maria, begin to disrobe yourself; here, Jane and Mary assist the young lady."

MARIA.—"Oh! No! No! I can't be stripped, I didn't know you did that," blushing more than ever, and pushing the servants away from her. "Give me the things and I will retire to make the change but not before you all."

PRESIDENT.—"Already disobeying the regulations; you must strip this instant or the birch will be used without mercy, and we shall see if you are so fond of it."

MARIA.—"Ah! I beg your pardon, but—you really must excuse me from undressing before so many."

Here the President takes up a most formidable rod, made of a thick bunch of long birch twigs, elegantly tied together with red and blue ribbons, and giving a sign, Jane and Mary, assisted by four or five others, pounced upon the victim, dragged her to the ladder, and in spite of desperate struggles, secured both ankles and wrists with cord which were passed through the rings of the ladder, and Miss Maria found herself quite helpless before she was well aware of what was going to be done.

PRESIDENT, advancing to the victim rod in hand.—"Ah! I see, this is a case of serious obstinacy; rip off that dress, and pull up her skirts, the sooner we begin to initiate her a little the better."

They all help to tear off the dress, etc., the victim is scarlet with shame, and shrieks out, "Ah! Oh! Pray don't, I've been deceived, I'm not a girl at all, don't expose me," tears of mortification running down his cheeks.

PRESIDENT, authoritatively.—"Stop, then, who may you be, are you a male or a hermaphrodite?"

The spectators all laugh at this question, and seeing his tongue-tied confusion, cry out, "Go on, go on, Miss Coote, give the impudent fellow a taste of your tickler, he must confess everything, and take an oath of secrecy or we'll whip him to death."

VICTIM.—"My God, what a scrape I'm in, these devils of girls will murder me. Oh! let me go, and I will swear never to tell anything."

PRESIDENT.—"Plenty of time for that bye-and-bye, you're not going to get off quite as easily after your impudent conspiracy with Lady Lucretia; you shall both see each other well whipped; you won't be shocked at seeing the bottom we know you are so well acquainted with. You're secure enough. Jane, prepare Sister Lucretia for punishment, so that he may know what to expect for himself."

LUCRETIA.—"Ah! No! I never meant anything but a little fun, you know I wished to birch him, and this is the only way I could manage it."

PRESIDENT.—"Very well, Miss, we'll take that all into consideration, and perhaps let you put the finishing touches to his bottom bye-and-bye. Put her posteriors in the stocks, Jane."

Leaving the young gentleman securely fixed to the ladder, they seize upon his ladylove, who knows better than to resist, and in a few moments Frank has the pleasure of seeing her blooming bottom and beautiful legs projecting from the wooden stocks in which she is so fixed that only the nether half of her person can be seen.

PRESIDENT.—"Now Mdlle. Fosse will administer a proper

correction for the insult she has put upon the Club by introducing a person of another gender amongst us."

MDLLE. FOSSE, who has armed herself with an excellent bum-tickler of well-pickled birch.—"I don't think the impudent hussey was half punished when we admitted her, or the soreness of her bottom would surely have kept her out of this." Then whack—whack—whack—she gives four very smart strokes with great deliberation. "How do you like that, is my arm heavier than Miss Coote's?"

LUCRETIA, screams and kicks her legs about in great pain.— "Ah! Oh! Oh! I beg—I beg pardon, indeed I thought a young gentleman would be a most agreeable accession to the Club. Oh! Ah! how you cut, it's dreadful!" as the blows continue to fall with great effect and precision, each one leaving its long crimson and blood-red marks and weals.

MDLLE. FOSSE.—"I must be quick, as it will take some time to punish Master Frank. I hope he is enjoying the sight of your castigation; is it as nice as it was before? let us know when your prurient ideas are satisfied by that feeling of sensuous pleasure you told us you experienced then," touching the tips of her birch in under her exposed pussey, and between the tender inner surfaces of her upper thighs.

The male victim's face was flushed with excitement at the sight of his lady's punishment, every blow seemed to thrill through his system, and put him into such a state of feeling as he had never experienced before, bringing out all the sensuality of his disposition as he watched the scene with rapt attention.

Mademoiselle plies her rod so vigorously that the blood soon begins fairly to trickle over Lucretia's bottom and thighs. "Ah! Oh! I shall faint. I shall die!" she sobs, writhing and twisting beautifully under the continued flagellation.

The President here comes forward with her rod saying, "I think Master Frank is longing to taste what it is like; pin up his skirts as decently as possible. I only want to see his bottom, we don't want the other thing introduced to our notice."

Frank was so absorbed in watching the beautiful sight of

Lucretia's whipping that he never knew his own skirts were pinned up till a tremendous whack on his own bum awaked him in a most lively manner to a sense of his forlorn condition. He winces and bites his lips, the tears starting to his eyes, and an extra crimson flushing over his face, all convince the spectator of his renewed humiliation. Again and again the President makes her blows sound through the apartment, but not till seven or eight weals have been raised on his posteriors will Master Frank gratify them by the least approach to a cry.

PRESIDENT, with a tremendous crack which fairly draws the blood.—"I'll make you beg our pardon, sir. Will you ever insult us by coming here as a girl again?"

Frank, trying to bear it pluckily, and ashamed to cry out before a lot of girls, writhes his buttocks in agony, and still bites his lips in silence till they fairly bleed.

PRESIDENT.—"Obstinate, eh, so much the more fun for us, my boy; will you beg pardon, and swear never to tell anyone of this spree of yours?" cutting his white bottom with all her might, each blow scoring the flesh and making it raw.

FRANK.—"Ah! I must call out, it's awful. Oh! don't quite murder me ladies. Ah—r—r—re!"

PRESIDENT.—"Will you come here again, you impudent fellow, will you take the oath now to keep our secret?" keeping him in constant agony by her well-applied strokes.

Frank's cries and Lucretia's sobs, in addition to the sight of two well-pickled bottoms, made the ladies all quite excited; each one takes up her birch, and as the President and Mademoiselle retire, they relieve each other in short spells of birching on the posteriors of the two victims, till at last Lucretia is nearly spent; she gets oblivious to pain, and seems lost in a kind of lethargic stupor. They let her down, and apply restoratives, which soon bring her to herself again, whilst Frank, who has been imploring for mercy, and praying to be sworn to secrecy for some minutes past, is at last allowed to take the required oath, but is greeted with renewed laughter when he begs pitifully to be released and allowed to go home.

"Ha! Ha! he thinks we shall let him go now, he can't object to Lucretia finishing him off, when she's a little recovered."

FRANK.—"It was all her fault, I should never have come, only she assured me of a warm welcome."

PRESIDENT, laughing.—"That's good, ladies, is it not? And you can't say we haven't given you one, but it must be warmer still before we let you go."

Lucretia swallows some stimulating cordial, and with sparkling eyes announces herself as ready to assume the rod; they hand her an elegant new one, and she takes her position, evidently minded to give him a little after the fashion of Louise Van Tromp's style of birching. "Do you," said she, "dare to insinuate that I tempted you to come here, sir?" flourishing the rod over her head so that he could hear it hissing through the air.

FRANK, all of a tremble.—"Ah! Ah! Lucretia, will you too prolong my torture, now I have promised everything."

Lucretia, bringing down her rod in earnest, makes his bottom wince and writhe under the stroke as she says, "Then you don't withdraw that insinuation, sir." Whisk—whisk—whisk, each blow harder than the last, and getting excited more and more, as the cuts seem to make the blood boil more tumultuously in her own veins, "Is it not true that you ravished me, sir? these ladies know all about your shameful conduct to me."

FRANK, in agony and desperate at this renewed torture.— "Ah! Oh! Ah! I'm hanged if I own all that, why you know you had my—my—you know what I mean in your hand first."

LUCRETIA, angrily.—"Don't mention the disgusting monster," cutting him desperately across the shoulders, "hold your wicked tongue, sir, if you are only going to asperse my character," again paying her attention to his raw-looking bum.

Frank, who has now lost his false hair by twisting his head about too much, looks a little more manly, but is a very fair youth withal, although his rump is not so finely developed as it would have been in a girl.

Lucretia, who feels all the stimulating warmth of her own flagellation, cuts away in fury. "See, see," she cries, "that unmentionable thing of his is quite rampant, and sticks out under his shirt in front, it's impossible to hide the disgusting creature." Striking more and more round his buttocks, which so disarranges his shirt that we continually get glimpses of a very formidable-looking weapon projecting six or seven inches from a bed of curly light hair at the bottom of his belly, the youth's eyes roll in a kind of erotic frenzy, and every thought of pain and shame has evidently given away to his sensuous feelings as he writhes and twists his bottom in a most lascivious manner at every stroke. The flagellatrix is also beside herself, the sight of his bleeding bottom and erotic emotion increases her fury more and more. "Ah!" she cries, "he not only tries to make me out worse than himself, but see how insultingly he is exposing himself to us all!" cutting the next stroke so as to reach the offending member. This she does again and again, causing such intense pain and excitement that at last the poor fellow shouts out, "Oh! Oh! My God! I shall burst, it's awful, and yet gives most delicious sensations! Ah—r—re! Ah—r—r—re! Oh! Oh!" and then he seems to die away in an excess of voluptuous emotion.

Lucretia suspends her rod for a few instants and then suddenly wakes him up again with two or three tremendous whacks upon his sore posteriors, exclaiming, "Wake up, sir, we've had enough of that, perhaps you will now withdraw your insinuations against me; did you not take advantage of my confusion, when I found you so exposed in the garden?" following up her question by a lively application of her rod, till the blood fairly trickles down Master Frank's thighs.

FRANK, again in awful pain, and ashamed to think how he has been exposed, now his erotic excitement has passed off for the moment.—"Ah! Ah! you she-devil, who could believe you could cut me up so after your loving caresses and assertions of your affection for me. Ah! Miss Coote, save me from her, have mercy ladies!" the tears of shame and agonized mortification running down his crimson face.

LUCRETIA.—"Not yet, you impudent boy; will you withdraw

your assertions about me, or I will literally skin your bottom before you get let off."

FRANK.—"Oh! Oh! how cruel of you Lucretia, to force me to tell a lie, how can I?" writhing under the shower of smarting strokes, and evidently beginning to experience the return of his voluptuous feelings.

LUCRETIA.—"Your cries are delightful. I enjoy it so much more, knowing how we love each other. Will—will you withdraw your wicked assertions? You have made these ladies think me a monster of lasciviousness. Do you hear, sir?" cutting well up under the crack of his bottom, so that the tips of the birch might sting him in the tenderest and most private parts.

VICTIM.—"Ah! Oh! Oh! My God! you'll kill me," seeming almost ready to faint with the suddenly excruciating pain.

LUCRETIA.—"Then why do you obstinately persist in refusing the satisfaction I ask of you, and say I want to make you tell lies, you wicked fellow, I'll murder you with the birch if you don't retract your vile insinuations," cutting him terribly everywhere she fancies he can feel most.

FRANK, in terrible agony.—"Oh! Oh! What—what must I say—all those stories about us are quite untrue, we never did anything wrong," writing about and hardly knowing what he says in his anxiety to get away from his torture.

LUCRETIA, with a furious blow which almost takes his breath away.—"Hold, hold, now, sir, you go to the other extreme; I only want you to confess you took advantage of me; your brain is confused, what a strange thing that after all this whipping and wealing the blood should still fly to your head."

FRANK, sobbing with mortification.—"Indeed—indeed, I remember now, how I put my hand under your clothes, when you were so overcome you could not resist me. Ah! Oh! Oh! Let me off, you never need fear I shall tell the secret of my own humiliation!"

He is fairly broken down, Lucretia drops her worn-out birch as tears of sympathy rise in her large loving eyes, and she sobs, "Poor fellow, poor fellow, what made you so obstinate?"

PRESIDENT.—"Let him down, and make him kneel before me and beg our pardon for the indelicate scandal he has caused amongst us, as I can feel and see what painful emotions the sight has caused in every lady's breast."

He is released, and Frank, humbly kneeling, declares his sorrow for having so shamefully intruded upon our private proceedings and again promises faithfully to keep our secret, and begs with fresh tears in his eyes to be allowed to remain a member after his painful initiation.

This was most favourably received, and I soon found out that Lady Clara was at the bottom of a plot for introducing the male element into our society.

I hastily closed the séance, and never knew how or what means they used to ease his sore bottom, but next day, by advice of Mdlle. Fosse, I intimated to them all a dissolution of the Club, as I could not possibly join in or allow my house to be used for birching orgies in connection with the opposite sex. My next and last letter on this subject will relate more nearly to myself.

Yours affectionately,
ROSA BELINDA COOTE.

LETTER X.

_____

My dear Nellie,—

I have found a curious letter from a lady amongst grandfather's papers, so begin this letter with a copy of it.

Dear Sir Eyre,—

We live in an age so dissolute that if young girls are not kept under some sort of restraint and punished when they deserve it, we shall see bye-and-bye nothing but women of the town, parading the streets and public places, and, God knows, there are already but too many of them!

When fair means have been used, proper corrections free from cruelty should be administered.

What punishment, and at the same time more efficacious, than birch discipline?

Physicians strongly recommend to punish children with birch for faults which appear to proceed from a heavy or indolent disposition, as nothing tends more to promote the circulation of the blood than a good rod made of new birch, and well applied to the posteriors.

I may add my own opinion that the rod is equally good in its effects on quick, excitable temperaments. With such children the sense of shame and exposure (if corrected before other children) adds greatly to the humiliation caused by the smarting strokes on their bare flesh and makes a lasting impression on their imaginative sensibilities.

The parent who uses the rod with discretion is infinitely more respected and reverenced by his children than a more indulgent one.

Birch breaks no bones, and therefore can do no great harm; the harm it does is very trifling when put in comparison with the evils which it can prevent.

I know it is pretty well used among what are called genteel people, but in that class, where it is chiefly wanted, the children are entirely left to their depraved habits, and from want of proper corrections become too often the shame of their parents.

Is it not better to chastise when she is yet young (for bad habits are generally contracted from the age of twelve to fifteen), than to see her, when grown up, taken to a house of correction for offences which a good whipping given with a birch rod might have prevented?

She is ruined body and soul by being thrown amongst the vilest possible human beings.

There are children so obstinate and of a nature so perverse that nothing but severe corrections will amend them.

I know a young widow of fashion who has three nieces and two nephews, who live with her. They are all above twelve years old, except her own daughter, who is nearly seven.

One of the girls is tolerable, but the other two as well as the two boys are exceedingly mischievous. She is indeed a strict disciplinarian, and always punishes their faults with the birch, and though she is yet quite young (not above four and twenty), she manages the children as well as any experienced schoolmistress could.

The other day the second eldest girl, who is about fourteen, told her brother she could tell him how children were made. And indeed instructed him so well that the boy, who is thirteen, a few days after took very improper liberties with a pretty young girl of fifteen, who acts in the house as a waiting-maid to the widow.

The girl complained to her mistress, who having found out that her niece was as guilty, if not more so than the boy, sent the girl immediately for a fresh broom, wishing to give them what is called a thorough whipping.

She made two large slashing rods, with the greenest and strongest twigs she could pick out of the broom, and beginning with her niece, she pinned her shift to her shoulders and tied her hands in front to prevent her from making a rear guard of her hands. She then whipped her posteriors and thighs as hard as she could, and continued whipping her without intermission, as long as she could hold the rod.

Having rested a few minutes she seized the boy, pulled his breeches down to his heels, and with the other rod she flogged him for ten minutes, and with such vigour of arm as made the young libertine kick and plunge like a colt, screaming in agony all the while.

For my part I think she acted in that instance very properly and such a correction may be hereafter of great service to these children, for it is better not to whip a child at all than not to make him feel well the stings of the birch.

I called last week on a friend of mine, an eminent mantua-maker in the city, whom I found in a violent passion.

On enquiring the cause, she told me that one of her apprentices had stolen a large silver spoon, and just as she was going to send her maid to gaol on suspicion she received a letter from an honest Jew, to whom the culprit had sold it, intimating he had suspected his customer, and followed the girl to her house, and offering to return the article.

"Now," said she to me, "I generally correct my apprentices with the birch, but I have just bought this horsewhip (showing me a large heavy carter's whip) to flog the hussey with. I will strip her and horsewhip her, till every bit of her skin is marked with it."

"Pray don't use that murderous thing," I expostulated in reply, "you might be punished for it; people have not yet forgotten Mother Brownrigg's case, who whipped her apprentices to death for the fun and cruelty of the thing."

It was with the utmost difficulty I could prevail upon her to substitute a good birch rod for that cruel whip. However, on my persistently representing to her the cruelty of chastising a girl with a horsewhip (although I am sorry to say I have actually seen it done in many families, where those in authority were inconsiderate and hasty in their tempers, and would use the first thing that came to hand), she consented to do the whipping with a good birch.

Domestic discipline, to be most effective, ought always to be carried out calmly, and all show of temper in inflicting punishment ought especially to be avoided, as likely to conduce to a want of respect in the delinquents.

A cart full of birch brooms, just cut from the trees, happening to pass by at that moment, she sent the servant to purchase a couple of them.

We both went upstairs to the back garret where the girl was confined. She appeared to me about fifteen, exceedingly pretty, with a beautiful white and delicate skin.

At the desire of my friend I stripped her of her clothes except her shift, and then the girl was ordered to seat herself on the floor, where the two brooms were thrown down in front of her, and select the finest pieces of birch herself, and tie them up into a rod, her mistress all the while pointing out particularly fine bits as most suitable for her thievish bottom, &c., and putting the girl into the greatest possible shame and confusion, the presence of a stranger like myself evidently adding immensely to her mortification.

When the rod was finished she tied her to one of the posts of the bed, and began to whip the young pilferer's posteriors and thighs with all her strength.

"Oh! you hussey!" she would exclaim, "will you ever steal anything again? Will you? Will you? Will you? I will teach you to be honest! I'll whip it into your system."

"Oh, God! Oh, gracious heaven! Oh, mistress! Oh, mistress!" screamed the girl, wriggling and twisting like a little devil on feeling the smarting cuts of the new birch. "Do forgive me, I will never steal any more for the rest of my life! Oh! Oh! Indeed I won't!"

But the mistress, foaming with rage, kept on flogging her with unremitting fury, till the rod was worn out, and she had to drop it from sheer exhaustion.

Then she called the servant, and ordered her to wash the girl's weals and bruises with some strong brine.

She means to give her every Saturday during a month just such another whipping. I think she is quite right to do so, as such corrections will deter the girl in all probability from ever stealing again.

When we left she was ordered by her mistress to amuse herself during the week by making four more good useful rods from the brooms which were left with her.

I have myself three daughters grown up, the eldest is about fourteen; she was addicted to telling lies, but I have whipped that quite out of her; my second daughter I have also entirely cured of some very dirty habits; but the youngest, who is about twelve, is not only idle and obstinate but exceedingly mischievous. I have made no impression upon her as yet, but am determined she shall feel the stings of the birch every day, if necessary, till she amends.

Believe me, dear Sir Eyre,
Yours faithfully,
MARY WILSON.

Now for my own adventure promised in the last. You will remember that in giving some account of my establishment, I mentioned Charlie the page, brother to my favourite servant Jane.

Well, he was such a nice boy as to be a universal favourite in the house, just sixteen, beardless as a girl, with a soft voice and very willing and agreeable, in fact he was such a good-looking youth as to make quite an impression upon me, but I resolutely kept the secret buried in my own bosom.

In my second letter I told all about my regard for Jane, and it was often my practice, especially when I awoke too early of a bright summer's morning, to get up in my nightdress and slip unseen into Jane's chamber, to satisfy my restlessness by a luscious embrace in the arms of my favourite.

But one morning as I approached the door, which was slightly ajar, I heard a suppressed sigh, and cautiously peeping in, to my infinite astonishment saw Master Charlie with nothing but his shirt on, and that drawn up almost under his arms, on the top of his sister Jane, who was equally nude. His lips were pressed to hers in the ardour of coition, and her legs were thrown over his loins.

My first impulse was to withdraw as silently as I had come, but the luscious sight rooted me to the spot, and like Moses at the burning bush, I felt constrained to witness the wonderful sight. There was his youthful shaft, almost as big as that of Mr. Aubrey mentioned in my last; it looked as hard and smooth as ivory, and I was forced to fix my attention on its rapid pushing and withdrawing motion, which she seemed to encourage and meet by the heaving of her bottom to every rapid shove.

The door was close to the foot of the bed, and as they were quite unconscious of my presence, I knelt down to avoid being seen, and enjoy the voluptuous sight to the end.

I felt awfully agitated and all of a tremble, it was so new to me and unexpected, brother and sister. Ah! how they seemed to love and enjoy each other; they cling to each other in ecstasy, and the lips of her vagina seemed literally to cling to his shaft, holding on and protruding in a most luscious manner at each withdrawing motion, but it soon came to an end, as both died away in a mutual flood of bliss, whilst a warm gush from my own cunny bedewed my thighs with an overflow of what was as yet a truly maiden emission.

Hot, flushed and confused I silently withdrew from the scene unobserved, fully determined to punish Mr. Charlie for his incestuous intercourse with his sister, and if possible secure him for my own enjoyment.

The temptation was irresistible; the more I thought and strove to banish it from my thoughts, the more would my blood boil and throb through my veins at the thoughts of what I had seen, and must experience for myself. It was no use; I could not struggle against the fascination of the thing.

It was a Sunday morning. Mdlle. Fosse would go to Moorfields to her father confessor, and attend an afternoon lecture; so as soon as I had done luncheon I told Jane and the other two servants they might go out for the afternoon and return by half-past six or seven, as I would dispense with dinner if Margaret the cook would have something nice for supper, and Charlie could answer my bell if anything was wanted.

As soon as the house was clear, and I knew the cook liked the society of her pots and pans too much to think of leaving the precincts of the kitchen, I rang for my page, and ordered him to bring a lemon, some iced water, sugar, &c., and seeing that he had dressed himself with scrupulous care in case I summoned him, I said, "Charlie, I'm glad to see you are particular about your appearance, although there is no one at home."

CHARLIE, with great modesty.—"But you, Miss, are my mistress, and I always wish to show you the greatest possible respect even when you are quite alone."

ROSA.—"Indeed, sir, you profess great respect for me, and seem afraid hardly to lift your eyes, as if I was too awful to look at, but I have my doubts about your goodness; will you please fetch me a rather long packet you will find wrapped in paper on the library table."

He soon returned with the parcel, and I proceeded to open it as he stood before me, awaiting his dismissal or further orders. The paper was removed, and I flourished before his face (which rather flushed at the sight) a good long rod of fresh green birch, tied up with scarlet ribbons. "Do you know what this is for, sir?" I asked the astonished boy.

CHARLIE, in some little confusion.—"Ah! Oh! I don't know—unless it's what's used for whipping young ladies at school."

ROSA.—"And why not boys, you stupid?"

CHARLIE.—"Ah! Miss Rosa, you're making fun of me, they use canes and straps to boys—but—but—."

ROSA.—"Out with what you are going to say, I'm the only one that can hear it."

CHARLIE.—"Why—why—(turning quite scarlet), the thought came into my head that you might be going to whip me."

ROSA, with a smile.—"Well, that shows that at least you must know you have been doing something very bad; what is it?"

CHARLIE, in confusion.—"Oh! it was only a silly thought, and I didn't mean, I knew I deserved it."

ROSA.—"That's a clever answer, Master Charlie. Now, answer me, am I your only mistress?"

He cast down his eyes at his poser, but managed to stammer out, "Why, of course you are, Miss, as I am in your service alone."

ROSA.—"Now you bad boy, I prepared this rod on purpose for you; can't you guess what I saw early this morning in Jane's room?"

Charlie seemed as if shot; he fell on his knees before me, in the deepest shame and distress, covering his face with his hands, as he exclaimed, "Oh, God! how wicked of me, I ought to have known I should be sure to be caught. Oh! be merciful, Miss Rosa, don't expose us, it shall never happen again. Punish us anyhow rather than let anyone know of it."

ROSA.—"It's awful, but I'm inclined to keep your secret, and be merciful. Do you know that you are guilty of incest, and liable to be hung for it, both of you?"

CHARLIE, sobbing and crying.—"What, for that? I only went to kiss her last night, and then laid down by her side; somehow our kisses and the heat of our bodies led from one liberty to another, till—till—I stopped all night, and you found me there this morning."

ROSA.—"You shall both smart for this. I will whip you well myself to cure such obscenity, but if ever it happens again, remember you shall swing for it. Now, sir, off with your coat and vest, and let down your breeches with your behind toward me."

He was terribly shame-faced over doing as I ordered him, but too frightened of the consequences to remonstrate, and turning his back to me, he soon stood in his shirt, with his breeches well pulled down.

"Now, sir," I said, "draw up that chair and kneel upon it, with your face over the back, then just pull up your shirt so as to properly offer your uncovered rump to the rod. Mind you bear it like a man, and keep as I order you, or I will yet send for a constable to take you to goal."

CHARLIE, in a broken voice.—"Oh! Miss, I won't even call out if I can help it; punish me as much as you like, only don't betray us."

ROSA.—"Well sir, you'll find my hand rather heavy, but you must smart well for your awful crime," giving a couple of good stinging strokes which made their red marks, and suffused the white flesh of his pretty bum with a rosy tint all over.

"Will you? Will you? you bad boy, commit such incestuous wickedness with your sister again? There—there, I can't cut half hard enough to express my horror of the thing!" exclaimed I, striking every blow with great deliberation and force, till his skin was covered with bleeding weals, and I managed, as I walked round his posteriors in the exercise of the rod, to see that his face was a deep scarlet, but his lips were firmly closed; the sight of his bottom just beginning to trickle with blood so excited me that my arms seemed to be strengthened at every cut, to give a heavier stroke next time.

"Ah! Oh! Oh! I will never do it again. Ah—r—r—re! I can't keep my mouth shut any longer. It's awful! Oh! Oh! How it burns into my flesh!" as he was compelled to writhe and wriggle under my fearful cuts.

This went on for about twenty minutes; now and then I had to slacken a little for want of breath, but his sighs and suppressed cries urged me on; it was a most delicious sensation to me; the idea of flogging a pretty youth fired my blood so much more than if the victim had been a girl; the rod seemed to bind me in voluptuous sympathy with the boy, although I was in perfect ecstasy at the sight of his sufferings. At last I sank back on a sofa quite exhausted with my exertions, and presently found him kneeling in front of me, kissing my hand, which still held the birch, exclaiming, "Ah! Miss Rosa, how you have pickled me; but, oh! I'm sure to do something bad again to make you whip me another time, it's so beautiful I can't describe what I feel, but all the pain was at last drowned in the most lovely emotions."

ROSA, in a faint voice.—"Oh! Charlie, how wicked of you, there, you shan't kiss my hand, my foot is good enough for you to beg pardon of."

CHARLIE, in rapture.—"My God! Miss Rosa, may I kiss that dainty little trotter of yours?" seizing one of my feet, and pressing his lips to my slightly exposed calf.

His touch was like a spark to a train of powder, I sank quite back on the sofa in a listless state, leaving my leg at his mercy, and seemed unable to repel his liberties; I felt his roving hand on the flesh of my thighs under the drawers, but the nearer he approached to the sacred spot the less able was I to resist; his hands went higher and higher, the heat of unsatisfied desire consumed me. At last with an effort I whispered, "Oh! oh! for shame, Charlie, what are you doing? come let my leg go, I want to tell you something. Ah! the punishing of you has been the undoing of me, ah! I am indeed afraid of you," hiding my face in my hands just as he raised his beautiful scarlet visage close to mine, and one of my feet also just touched something projecting in front under his shirt. "Oh! Oh! what's that in front of you Charlie," I gasped.

"Oh, dear Miss, it's what Jane calls 'the boy,' and gives such pleasure that Aaron's rod could not equal its magic power," he said softly.

ROSA, hysterically.—"Oh! Oh! Charlie, will you be good and true to me, my life, my honour are in your power, you will never use my confusion, the secret that my impulsive nature cannot restrain. Ah! you naughty boy, it was the sight of your performance with your sister fired my imagination so that I determined to score your bottom well for you, but, alas, the sight has been too much for the sensuality of my disposition—."

I could not continue what I had to say, but the dear boy covered my face and bosom with kisses, his searching hands finding out and taking possession of all my secret charms, while I could not restrain my own hands from being equally free, and repaid his hot burning kisses with interest.

Our lips were too busy to give utterance to words; in short I surrendered everything to the dear boy, and we swam in the delights of love; of course I experienced the painful tension and laceration of my hymen, but all was soon forgotten in the flood of bliss which ensued.

His efforts exhausted him, and I had further recourse to the rod to procure myself a repetition of our joys, and lastly when I feared the dear youth might perhaps be seriously injured if I exacted from him more than nature could sustain, I prevailed upon him to use the birch on my own bottom, so as to keep my voluptuous sensations from abating.

Ah! the rod is delicious if skillfully applied after the delights of coition. The dear boy wanted to renew his attack, but I would not permit it, promising he should come to my room at night for another feast of love, but insisting upon his being rested for the present.

I enjoyed a most voluptuous liaison with my page for three or four years, till I was constrained to part with him on account of his manly appearance. By my advice and assistance he married well, entered into business, and became a thriving man. From time to time, as long as he lived, we secretly enjoyed the sweets of each other's society.

You have often wanted to know why I never married; the truth is, two things combined to prevent it. The first being my love of independence, and aversion to being subject to anyone, however I might love him; this I might perhaps have brought myself to give up, but the second reason was insurmountable. I could not get a new maidenhead, and positively gave up all idea of marriage without that article, so essential to all spinsters who enter the hymeneal state.

Poor Charlie died in the prime of his life, at thirty-five, but before his decease gave me a packet of papers relating to his amorous adventures, by which I find he was not very faithful to me, even when in my service, but *"de mortuous nil nisi bonum"* is my motto, I only know I loved him when I had him.

Perhaps someday I may put his memoirs into some shape for your perusal, but this letter is the finis of these selections from my own experience.

Believe me,
 Your affectionate friend,
  ROSA BELINDA COOTE.

BIRCHGROVE PRESS
Flagellant & Libertine Literature

Birchgrove Press specializes in producing new print and e-book editions of pre-1950s writings on sexual flagellation in English. Original editions of many of the books that we offer are difficult to obtain and are highly sought after. We are especially proud to offer new editions of rare Victorian flagellant texts such as *The Mysteries of Verbena House*, *Experimental Lecture by Colonel Spanker*, and *The Quintessence of Birch Discipline*. Birchgrove Press also produces new editions of libertine literature. We have published *Venus in the Cloister*, *The School of Venus*, *The Dialogues of Luisa Sigea*, and Isidore Liseux's translation of the Marquis de Sade's Justine (1791), *Opus Sadicum*, for example.

www.birchgrovepress.com

More books from

Birchgrove Press

Curiosities of Flagellation, a Series of Incidents, And Facts Collected by an Amateur Flagellant. Volumes I and II. First published in 1875 and 1880.

The Mysteries of Verbena House; or, Miss Bellasis Birched for Thieving - First published as two volumes in one in 1882.

Experimental Lecture by Colonel Spanker - One of the most notorious English flagellant novellas. First published in 1878-79. Includes *The Yellow Room*, first published 1891.

The Pleasures of Cruelty; Being a sequel to the reading of Justine et Juliette by the Marquis de Sade - first published as three volumes in one in 1886.

Swivia; or, the Briefless Barrister. The Extra Special Number of The Pearl - first reprint in over a century of the 1879 Christmas edition of *The Pearl: A Journal of Facetiæ and Voluptuous Reading* (1879-1880).

The Haunted House or The Revelations of Theresa Terence - first reprint in over a century of the 1880 Christmas edition of the *The Pearl: A Journal of Facetiæ and Voluptuous Reading* (1879-1880).

The Romance of Chastisement; or, Revelations of the School and Bedroom. - Written by St. George H. Stock. First published 1871.

The Flogging-Block An Heroic Poem in a Prologue and Twelve Eclogues by Algernon Charles Swinburne. A Transcription of The Original Holograph Manuscript Written at intervals between 1862 and 1881 - first publication of Swinburne's mock-heroic tribute to corporal punishment.

The Whippingham Papers - first published 1887. Most of the pieces were written by St. George H. Stock. Includes poems by Swinburne.

Raped on the Railway A True Story of a Lady who was First Ravished and then Chastised on the Scotch Express - first published in Paris in 1899.

*The Petticoat Dominant or Woman's Revenge The Autobiography
of a Young Nobleman as a Pendant to Gynecocracy by
M. Le Comte du Bouleau.* First published 1898.

*Gynecocracy. A narrative of the Adventures and Psychological
Experiences of Julian Robinson (afterwards Viscount
Ladywood) Under Petticoat-Rule, written by himself.*
First published in 1893.

*Stays and Gloves: Figure-Training and Deportment
by Means of the Discipline of Tight Corsets,
Narrow High-Heeled Boots, Clinging Kid Gloves,
Combinations, etc., etc.* First published in 1909.

*White Stains The Literary Remains of George Archibald
Bishop a Neuropath of the Second Empire.*
Written by magician and occultist Aleister Crowley.
First published 1898.

Snowdrops from a Curate's Garden.
Written by Aleister Crowley. First published 1904.

Miss Mary - English translation of a French flagellant
   novel written by Alphonse Momas. First published 1907.

Miss Grégor - English translation of a French flagellant
   novel written by Alphonse Momas. First published 1907.

Whipping as a Fine Art - Edwardian flagellant novel
   attributed to Charles Sackville. First published c. 1909.

*Les Mystères de la Maison de la Verveine: ou Miss Bellasis
   fouettée pour vol* - French translation of *The Mysteries
   of Verbena House*. First published in 1901. Facsimile edition.

*The Exhibition of Female Flagellants: Parts One and Two –
Two volumes in one.* First published c. 1780 - 1785.

Alraune - English translation of Hanns Heinz Ewers'
decadent novel. First published in German in 1911.

www.ingramcontent.com/pod-product-compliance
Lightning Source LLC
Chambersburg PA
CBHW071134200626
46817CB00018B/2946